THE SHADOWS OF HAVANA

Also by Craig Pennington

West of the Alleghenies
A Story of Survival During the Revolutionary War

2021 Royal Palm Literary Award
Best Published Book of the Year, 4th Runner-Up
Best Published Historical Fiction, Silver Medal Winner

§

The Heart of the Run
A Story of Scotland and Ireland

2022 Royal Palm Literary Award
Best Published Historical Fiction Gold Medal Winner

§

**Murder on
the Underground Railroad**
A Historical Thriller

"This is so much more than a mystery."
— Historical Novel Society

§

Dead Reckoning
A Caribbean Thriller

§

Volcano Wind
A Caribbean Caper

THE SHADOWS OF HAVANA

By
Craig Pennington

Copyright © 2024 by Craig A. Pennington
ISBN: 9798335628242
Independently published
All rights reserved. No part of this book
may be reproduced, scanned, or distributed in any
printed or electronic form without permission.
Printed in the United States of America
First Printing: September 2024

Special thanks to Michael Brown
and Scott DeWolfe for permission to use the link
to their *Walker Evans Havana 1933* catalog

Associated Press article
Long-Hidden Photos Unravel a Mystery
reprinted with permission of
Wright's Media 2024

Cover art from postermywalls.com

Although this work is inspired by actual historical events, certain events, dialogue, and characters were created for the purpose of fictionalization. Names, characters, places, and incidents either are the product of the author's imagination or are used fictitiously. Any resemblance to actual persons, living or dead, events, or locales is entirely coincidental.

For Claudia
whose masterful exhibition
inspired this novel,
and Dink
who thankfully saved everything

Table of Contents

Prologue 1

One 12

Two 30

Three 41

Four 50

Five 61

Six 77

Seven 85

Eight 102

Nine 117

Ten 128

Eleven 137

Twelve 149

Thirteen 161

Fourteen 175

Fifteen 183

Sixteen 194

Seventeen 201

Eighteen 207

Nineteen	214
Twenty	221
Twenty-One	229
Twenty-Two	239
Twenty-Three	247
Twenty-Four	254
Twenty-Five	262
Twenty-Six	274
Afterword	286
Long-Hidden Photos Unravel a Mystery	290
References	293
Special Thanks	295
The Author	296

THE SHADOWS OF HAVANA

Prologue

February, 1962
Sloppy Joe's Bar
Key West, Florida

A BEAD OF SWEAT trickled down Toby Bruce's nose and dripped on the faded typewritten page in his hand. He wiped his brow with a large handkerchief, his damp fingers smudging the ink on the paper in the process. Frustrated, he pressed the sheet against his trousers, attempting to salvage the text.

"It's too damn hot in here," Toby muttered, turning to his wife, Betty, who stood beside him in the stifling storage room at the back of Sloppy Joe's Bar. Out front, the bar was quiet and devoid of customers except for one old man asleep at a corner table.

Betty pushed a decrepit cardboard box toward Toby with her foot, stirring a cloud of dust that danced in the rays of sunlight streaming through the high window.

Her voice carried a note of weariness as she suggested, "Let's finish this box and call it a day. It'll be cooler tomorrow."

Seated on uncomfortable metal chairs and surrounded by dusty boxes, Toby and Betty [1] had spent the week sifting through an assortment of Ernest Hemingway's decaying personal effects with his fourth wife and widow, Mary. She had come to Key West after Hemingway's suicide the previous July to claim items she believed important.

This collection had been untouched for two decades, ever since Ernest's second wife, Pauline, demanded that he remove his belongings from their home on Whitehead Street as he embarked on his new life in Cuba with his soon-to-be third wife, Martha Gellhorn.

Termites had ravaged the old cardboard boxes, reducing them to crumbling remnants. On previous days, their efforts had uncovered boxes containing the detritus of years of an adventurous, disorganized, and overly indulgent life.

---

1 Telly 'Toby' Bruce (1910—1984) met Ernest Hemingway in 1929, later becoming his right hand man, confidant, and drinking companion. Bruce moved to Key West in 1935 to remodel Hemingway's house on Whitehead St. He married Laura Elizabeth 'Betty' Moreno (1918—1994) in 1943. Betty worked as a librarian and historian for the Monroe County Library. They had two children, Benjamin Curry 'Dink' Bruce and Linda Bruce.

However, there were also treasures hidden among the clutter.

In one box, Toby discovered a dozen never-before-seen snapshots Hemingway had taken during his African safari in 1933. In another, they found a stained brown notebook amid bullfighting tickets and newspaper clippings. Inside was Hemingway's first short story, about a fictional trip to Ireland, written when he was ten.

Mary Hemingway showed no interest in the photos or the short story, but Toby recognized their historical importance and set them aside.

Today, Mary had excused herself from their work after lunch, feigning a headache that confined her to the coolness of the La Concha Hotel.

As always, Toby and Betty bore the brunt of the labor. Toby had long been Hemingway's right-hand man, chauffeur, and drinking companion, ready to lend a hand, mix a drink, or mend a wall. Such were their roles in Key West and Cuba for the past twenty-five years.

Toby brushed a stray curl of hair clinging to his damp forehead and peeled his soaked shirt away from his thin chest. He pried open the box Betty had nudged his way, discovering a jumble of loose papers devoid of any discernible order.

Delving deeper into the box, Toby retrieved a large, faded envelope stained with watermarks. Tied shut with a worn red string looped around a paper button. Unwinding the string, he loosened the flap, allowing a stack of curling 8x10 black and white photographs to spill onto the table. Among the photos were shots of people queued for bread, fruit vendors with carts laden with melons, and glimpses into impoverished homes. The collection grew, showcasing a destitute family clothed in rags, a sailboat anchored in the harbor, and a striking young woman who stared directly into the camera.

"These are all from Cuba," Toby stated, recognizing the scenes from his years accompanying Hemingway between Key West and the island. "They're good, aren't they?"

Betty responded in a noncommittal tone, "I suppose."

Toby held a picture of a man, apparently a vagabond, asleep on a park bench, head lolling gracelessly against his upturned palm.

"This one makes me think of *To Have and Have Not*," he mused with the faintest trace of wistfulness. "Don't you think?"

"What about it?" Mary asked. She never appreciated that novel, considering it far too violent and dark.

" 'You know how it is there early in the morning in Havana with the bums still asleep against the walls of the buildings; before even the ice wagons come by with

ice for the bars?' " Toby quoted by heart the opening line of Hemingway's novel.

"I suppose…" Betty said again.

Toby flipped to the next photograph, his breath catching in his throat. "Oh, my God!" Betty exclaimed, recoiling in horror.

In Toby's trembling hands, a photograph depicted a man with his throat brutally slit from ear to ear. The victim's eyes bulged obscenely, distended tongue protruding in a wordless grimace of agony.

Hastily, he shuffled the print to the back of the stack, only to reveal a more gruesome image. It showed a lifeless body, postmortem incisions dissecting his chest, eyes swollen shut.

The man had been beaten to death.

Unable to bear the sight, Betty turned away. Each photograph in the grisly series seemed to outdo the previous one in raw, sadistic violence.

Toby placed the stack on the table and took a breath. He was certain Hemingway had not taken these photos. They were professional, studied, and intense, not the snapshots Hemingway loved to pose for. In their own morbid way, each photograph illustrated a dark tale shrouded in mystery and violence.

"How did anything like this get mixed in with Papa's stuff?" Toby asked.

"They're horrible," Betty said instead of answering.

Disturbed by the haunting images they had uncovered, Toby delved into the depths of the box. All that remained was a faded envelope laced with termite holes. A familiar name in the upper corner caught his eye—Hotel Ambos Mundos, the hotel Hemingway called home during his early years in Havana.

"This is Papa's handwriting on the back," Toby stated. "It says: *loaned $25*. Someone else addressed the envelope, though. They misspelled Hemingway."

Gently opening the envelope flap, he removed a note written in pencil on fragile Western Union stationary.

"Listen to this," he whispered, holding the small slip of paper up to the light. "*'I have some pictures tonight and will have more tomorrow. Also I will change my mind and take a loan of ten or fifteen dollars from you if you still feel like that...My telephone is F6631; Will you call me if you come in. W. Evans.'*"

"Huh!" Betty grunted.

"What?" Toby asked, recognizing that his wife had information to impart. "Do you know that name?"

Ever the astute librarian, Betty tapped her chin with a dirty finger. "W. Evans...pictures must mean photographs...It has to be Walker Evans! I thought the scenes in Havana were familiar. Walker Evans. You know he photographed sharecropper families in the South during the Depression."

"I guess...Was it well-known?"

"Yes," Betty nodded, her tone brightening as the details surfaced. "It wasn't his book alone. It was a collaboration with James Agee. You know him, Toby. He wrote the screenplay of that Humphrey Bogart movie you like so much, *The African Queen*? But *Let Us Now Praise Famous Men* was his masterpiece. Walker Evans did all of the photography for it. Made them both famous."

"John Huston wrote and directed *The African Queen*..."

"With James Agee, Toby. You, of all people, should know that."

Ignoring the playful jab, Toby slowly sifted through the stack of photos again, his mind trying to make sense of it all.

"Why in the world would Papa have Walker Evans's prints mixed in with his stuff? When would their paths have ever crossed?"

"I don't know," Betty said. "I do remember there being another book Evans collaborated on back in the early 30s. It was about Machado and the terrible things happening in Cuba. Papa had a copy of the book, although I don't remember him ever mentioning Walker Evans."

"It makes sense," Toby agreed. "It's the right timeframe for these other photos of Havana. And the dead men look like the work of Machado's goons." Toby paused, then asked, "When was Machado overthrown?"

Her encyclopedic memory worked well despite the years of hard drinking. "Nineteen thirty-three, I believe."

"Could Papa and Evans have met? Papa was definitely there in '33. It was the same year he went to Africa. The same year as Jane's accident..." Toby stopped talking, his mouth hanging open with sudden insight. "Do you realize what we have here? These could be unknown Walker Evans photos. Who knows how much they might be worth."

"First, we have to find out who owns them," said Betty.

Ignoring the ownership issues, Toby asked, "Why doesn't anyone know this? And why would Evans give Papa these particular photos?"

Betty shrugged. "Perhaps Evans feared Machado's Secret Police would never allow them to leave Cuba. Look at these dead men, Toby. Machado would have done anything to keep the world from knowing what he was doing. There can be only one answer. Walker Evans must have believed Machado would try to prevent these images from leaving Cuba, and he gave them to Papa in case something happened."

Toby shook his head. "If Evans thought Machado would prevent these pictures from leaving Cuba, perhaps he was worried about more than that. Maybe he was in danger, himself."

"Yes," Betty agreed, a chill running down her spine despite the oppressive heat, "he *would* have been in danger. Machado would not hesitate to murder anyone to keep the atrocities of his regime secret. I am sure Walker Evans feared for his very life…"

☙

June, 1933
Hotel Ambos Mundos
Havana, Cuba

"Go!" Hemingway thundered, pointing at the tall double windows as a flash of lightning illuminated Havana.

A hard voice from the hallway shouted, "This is the police, Señor Hemingway! Open up!"

I took a deep breath, opened the windows, and examined the brick ledge beyond. The curtains blew in, rain pelted my face and spattered on the floor.

What the hell was I thinking? I can't do this! My life-long fear of heights held me frozen in place.

Another hard bang rattled the door. "Señor Hemingway!"

"A minute, goddammit!" Hemingway shouted back. His look told me that I either climbed out the window or he would throw me out. "Go, Walker! Go to the next room. The windows are never locked. I'll meet you at the *Anita*. I'll be damned if they get their hands on those photos!"

I don't know where the courage came from. It had been a long day: I had been abducted in broad daylight, languished for hours in a prison cell, and faced the murderous head of the Secret Police. I was tired, frightened, and pissed off.

With one feeble smile for Dorothy, I tucked the oversized envelope under my belt, buttoned my coat, and stepped onto the narrow ledge over the railing. Pressing my back against the slick, rain-soaked wall, my fingers dug into the smallest masonry joint.

Rain beat furiously against my face, and each lightning flash left glowing orbs swimming in my eyes. Half-blinded by the storm, I inched along the ledge, my heart pounding. The wind whipped my clothes, threatening to snatch me from the building and hurl me to the pavement five stories below.

Gathering my quickly evaporating strength, I slid sideways the last few feet to the adjacent hotel room. I didn't know if it was occupied or not.

There was no point in being subtle. I pushed my back against the windows.

They didn't budge.

I was trapped.

One

May, 1933
New York City
Six Weeks Earlier

THE HARSH JANGLE of the telephone finally registered, waking me from a deep sleep. A dull throbbing ache pounded relentlessly behind my eyes as I fumbled for the receiver. My parched lips craved a soothing sip of cool water.

"What?" I croaked. Holding the handle in one hand, I massaged my temple with the other.

"Fancy a trip to Cuba, Walker?" The voice on the other end of the line was far too chipper for the ungodly hour of 10 a.m. It belonged to Ernestine Evans, friend, publicist, and editor-at-large for J.B. Lippincott, one of the country's most esteemed publishing houses.

"What?" The question emerged less aggressively this time, the sharpness of my initial irritation tempered by the confusion that muddled my throbbing brain.

"You still in bed?"

"It was a long night," I muttered, my mind clouded with memories of the self-indulgent bender my friend, the artist Ben Shahn, and I had embarked upon. The evening had been intended as a memorial of sorts, a final sendoff to the old bastard who had passed from this world two days prior. Ben, ever the consummate host, knew all the right people in the city, effortlessly gaining us admittance to the most exclusive speakeasies in town.

Apparently reading my mind through the telephone line, Ernestine said, "By the way, condolences on your father's passing."

"What about Cuba?" I asked, unwilling to discuss the man I had not spoken to in years. Still, I was somewhat surprised that the news of his death had reached Ernestine's ears. Her knack for knowing things others did not is what made her such a force in the publishing world.

"We, you and I, that is, are having lunch today with Carleton Beals. Ever heard of him?"

"No," I lied. Of course, everyone in the New York literary circles knew the name Carleton Beals. I had never met the man but was familiar with his work. My new friend Diego Rivera illustrated Beals's last book, *Mexican Maze*, which details the author's journey in post-revolutionary

Mexico. Critics called it a searing work of impressionistic prose and radical politics.

"Well," Ernestine continued as if my answer was irrelevant to our discussion, "get up, clean up, sober up, and meet us at Sardi's at one."

Before I could refuse, she abruptly hung up.

Ernestine Evans [2] (no relation, thank God) was a force of nature. Large, opinionated, and animated by endless energy, she dominated the publishing world, boasting friendships with literary luminaries like Gertrude Stein and Virginia Woolf. She often reminded me of my mother—an equally formidable woman yet lacking Ernestine's warmth.

I couldn't refuse her, even if I had wanted to. Four years earlier, Ernestine almost single-handedly catapulted Diego Rivera into the limelight with a lavishly produced volume showcasing his frescoes. Now, she was determined to find me a substantial paying gig—an endeavor that, given my current financial circumstances, I could not afford to ignore.

With a groan of resignation, I dragged myself from the tangled depths of my bed and stumbled into the bathroom. A blast of icy water from the

---

2 Ernestine Evans (1889—1967) was an American journalist, editor, author and literary agent. Evans authored the first English-language book on the famed Mexican muralist Diego Rivera, establishing both their reputations in the literary world.

showerhead did much to revive my senses, washing away the remnants of the previous night and the lingering ache behind my eyes.

Two hours and three cups of strong coffee with milk later, I emerged from the townhouse on Bethune Street. My friend Ben had graciously allowed me to take temporary residence while I endeavored to get my feet beneath me. Don't get me wrong—I wasn't a freeloader. I had enough money trickling in from various odd jobs to help pay my way, but not nearly enough to secure my own place. Not in this city.

Ben was a great friend and had rescued me more than once.

The stiff breeze off the Hudson added a crispness to the early May morning, and the wet streets glistened under the bright sunlight. I stepped around the few remaining puddles from the previous day's showers. Overhead, a brilliant blue sky beckoned, the sun's warmth already beginning to chase away the lingering chill.

I was glad to be wearing my dark brown double-breasted gaberdine. Out of style and slightly worn, it would pass inspection if the restaurant lights were low. After all, I didn't want to appear needy.

The subway ride uptown was a smokey, rattling affair, the screech of the train echoing off the tiles as it hurtled through the tunnels. Each stop added a fresh influx of passengers into the rapidly filling car. By the time we reached the Times Square station, the air was thick with stale smoke and sweat, the press of bodies almost suffocating in its intensity.

On the surface, I emerged into a sea of humanity, a mass of bodies flooding the sidewalks. I inhaled deeply, grateful for the relatively clean air, before fighting against the flow toward 44th Street.

As Times Square loomed into view, I paused to absorb the three blocks of chaotic beauty. Billboards and neon lights filled all available space, towering overhead in a dizzying jumble as if thrown against the buildings by a tornado. At the Broadway split, one gargantuan billboard advertisement touted the virtues of Pepsodent toothpaste. Directly below it, Coca-Cola promised to 'bounce you back to normal.' The irony of the juxtaposition made me smile.

On 7th Avenue, a massive poster hailed *42nd Street* as the year's best movie. Another vying for attention announced the upcoming release of *Gold Diggers of 1933*, starring the always elegant Dick Powell. It promised extravagant Busby Berkley numbers and a romantic storyline unlike any you have ever seen.

I spun in a slow circle, wishing I had thought to bring my camera. I loved the angles, the sheer immensity and power of it all. So many potential photographic studies are crammed into this vibrant space.

In these few chaotic blocks, the American story unfolds in all its gaudy splendor. Only a photograph could truly capture the essence of this place. The architecture, the signage, the overwhelming grandeur of it all was much more meaningful to me than the staid photos of the Brooklyn Bridge I had taken for my friend Hart Crane's epic poem. [3]

Times Square was the heart of the city.

If only there weren't so many damn people to mar the beauty, I mused. Then, to place an exclamation point on my thoughts, a woman carrying an armload of packages banked off me, continuing on her way without apologizing.

At that moment, the allure faded, and I was faced with grimy sidewalks despoiled with tobacco stains and pigeon droppings, petrified chewing gum, and cigarette butts.

With a heavy sigh, I turned west on 44th and approached the red canopied entrance of Sardi's.

---

3 Harold Hart Crane (1899—1932) was a poet whose stylized and complex form cemented him in the avant-garde literary scene for a time. The epic poem, *The Bridge* was published in 1930 to mixed reviews.

It was five minutes till one on May 4th, 1933, a day that held the promise of change, a day that would forever alter the course of my life.

I handed my battered fedora to the hatcheck girl in the foyer and pocketed the claim stub. It took a moment for my eyes to adjust to the dim interior of the restaurant. Every table on the main floor was occupied, the clinking of glasses and murmur of voices swelling into a cacophonous smoke-filled cloud.

Carleton Beals [4] sat alone in a secluded banquette beneath a wall packed with Alex Gard's caricatures. As I approached, weaving between the tightly spaced tables, Beals looked up. His rugged features shifted subtly, the strong jawline tightening as the corner of his mouth twisted into a sardonic smirk, as though he already regretted agreeing to this meeting.

We shook hands without introducing ourselves. His grip was firm, as if he hoped I would challenge his hand strength. Despite some greying at his temples, Beals appeared younger than his photos. He was several inches taller than my

---

4 Carleton Beals (1893—1979) was an American journalist, writer, historian, and political activist with a special interest in Latin America. Beals wrote over 200 magazine articles and 45 books on history, geography, and travel.

modest five-foot-seven and ruggedly handsome with broad shoulders and the weathered tan of a man used to spending time in the sun. An African safari guide or a tennis pro would have the same look.

"Ernestine not here yet?" I asked as we sat across the table from each other. It felt like we were already engaged in competition.

Beals shrugged indifferently. "I'm sure she wants to make an entrance. You know how she is, old man."

I chuckled politely, agreeing with the comment. For all the affected airs of continental sophistication—that impeccably tailored light gray wool suit which surely cost more than my monthly stipend, the rich blue silk tie, and coordinated pocket square—there was an undeniable charisma about the man.

"I believe we have a friend in common," I tried, opting for a different tack when he offered nothing more.

Beals raised an eyebrow but remained silent and aloof.

"Rivera," I said.

Mentioning Diego Rivera got more of a reaction. With a tilt of his head, Beals asked, "You know Diego?" as if questioning a man such as myself could ever be acquainted with an artist of Rivera's stature.

"Yes," I continued, ignoring his tone. "My friend, Ben Shahn, is assisting him with the Rockefeller mural in the RCA building. I've been photographing the progress periodically as it takes shape. Diego and I got to talking, and he expressed an interest in my work—especially the shots I captured of the Brooklyn Bridge."

We stopped talking when a waiter came to the table. I ordered a draft Yuengling. The hair of the dog was just what I needed. Thank God, or Roosevelt, for the recent revival of wine and real beer sales before the official end of Prohibition, scheduled for December.

When the frosty mug arrived, I took a long, grateful pull while Beals sipped his coffee. He smiled slightly at my obvious thirst.

"Diego's stubbornness," he said, delicately placing the coffee cup on its saucer, "will be his downfall. Rockefeller has already delayed the unveiling of the mural—it should have been this past Monday. All because of that damned article by the *Telegram*. I warned him that including Lenin's portrait would lead to disaster, no matter how deeply he tried to bury it. Now the entire project is at risk of being destroyed."

I didn't agree with his cynical assessment. Rivera had been commissioned to create a singular work of art for that grand space. As far as I was concerned, the Rockefellers had no right to dictate what could or could not be included, only the privilege of approving or rejecting his overall concept. However, that was the problem. Lenin's portrait was not in the original plan approved by the Rockefeller's board. He had added it out of spite.

Diego had been livid when the *World-Telegram* accused his creation of being anti-capitalist propaganda. Although openly a Communist, Diego didn't want his art to be labeled one way or the other. Lenin's portrait was a vindictive response to the article.

Beals was absolutely right on one point—Diego's hubris had jeopardized the entire project.

I was preparing to express my opinion when a commotion near the front door caught our attention.

Ernestine Evans had arrived.

We watched with amusement as she maneuvered her large frame toward us, stopping at half the tables along a circuitous path. In a voice that carried throughout the restaurant, Ernestine proclaimed her delight at encountering one acquaintance or another, bestowing enthusiastic hugs and air-kisses as she made her way across the room.

We both stood when she reached our secluded corner. Being on the outside, I was awarded a kiss on the cheek as a mass of fox stole, and a heavy dose of Shalimar engulfed me.

Ernestine slid in beside Beals. "My dear, Carleton!" she bubbled breathlessly. "I am so happy to see you. And you've had a chance to meet Walker. How dreadful of me running late. I worried you two wouldn't have anything to talk about!"

The same sardonic smile curved Beals's lips as he regarded her with an indulgent air. "We've been doing just fine, Ernestine."

"Oh, that's wonderful! We're off to a fine start, then."

"As a matter of fact," I added, "we discovered that Diego Rivera is a mutual friend."

"Well, of course he is," Ernestine effused with a mischievous twinkle in her eyes. "Diego knows every one of consequence in the art world! Shall we order? I'm famished…and buying, so eat up!"

My financial situation didn't allow for meals in any restaurant costing more than the Jewish deli on 14th Street, let alone Sardi's. I scanned the menu, my stomach growling in anticipation. Finally, I settled on the renowned Danska Special and another frosted mug of lager.

Beals ordered Eggs Benedict. Ernestine went all out with pork chops and a Virgin Bloody Mary.

When her drink arrived, Ernestine pulled a silver hip flask from her purse and added a liberal dose of vodka to the tall glass. She stirred the concoction with the celery stick and sipped. Evidently, the drink met her approval, for she downed two fingers before smiling innocently at me.

"So," she began, delicately licking the salt rim, "you two had a chance to get to know each other. That's wonderful. Did you discuss the project, Carleton?"

"No," Beals snapped. "And I'm not sure why we must."

"Well," Ernestine said evenly, raising one eyebrow in reproach, "I have talked it all over with Walter, and he agrees—Walker's unique style of photography would complement your book nicely."

I knew Walter was Walter Goodwin, art director at J.B. Lippincott and Co., based at the publishing house headquarters in Philadelphia. His name held considerable weight. I was thrilled to think a man in his position knew anything of my work.

God bless Ernestine Evans.

But, now I understood Beals's earlier hostility. He had no desire to involve any outsider in his project. I sympathized completely. Still, my curiosity had been sufficiently piqued.

"What is the book about?" I asked as innocently as I could. I didn't want to sound too desperate or too pushy.

Before Beals could respond, Ernestine said, "It's called *The Crime of Cuba*. Isn't that a perfect title? I came up with that!"

"Well—" Beals began to protest before Ernestine cut him off.

"Are you familiar with the man running Cuba—Gerardo Machado? He is a monster, a murderer, a beast of a man of no morals who is destroying Cuba."

Leaning forward on his elbows, Beals fixed his eyes directly at me. The man was very intense.

"They call him the *President of One Thousand Murders*," he said, his jawline tightening with conviction. "And the worst part is, through several US banks, our State Department supports him. My book, Evans, is an exposé condemning the United States' ongoing support of that man. He was elected in 1925 under the pretense of ushering in a new era of democracy, but since then, he's become a tyrant dead-set on establishing himself as president for life."

Beals was at full throttle. This subject was more than a writing assignment to him. He continued, "There's a growing insurrection taking root, determined to overthrow him—and they'll succeed if our government ends its support and the banks stop funneling funds to assist Machado in slaughtering his own people."

"When did you go to Cuba?" I asked.

"Last September. I lived in the country with the people for six weeks. Not in a tourist hotel. My book is comprehensive. It is a history, a social commentary, and a condemnation. It will speak for itself." This last sentence was directed at Ernestine.

Beals's commitment was clear. The set of his jaw and the intense way he looked directly at me convinced me of his passion.

This all sounded rather dangerous to me. "If your book is intended to expose both the regime and our government's part in keeping Machado in power, won't that put you squarely in the crosshairs on both sides?"

Ernestine laughed out loud and patted my arm. "Oh, Walker, you do have a way of stating the obvious. Of *course*, neither our government nor Machado wants this book published, but that is what journalism is all about. Thank God we live in a society where freedom of speech is our greatest right."

Still skeptical, I said, "That may be true here. Is it in Cuba? They certainly aren't protecting free speech. What will Machado think of this book? What will he think of my taking pictures to illustrate it?"

"No, you're right," Beals said. "He will *not* be happy. You shouldn't go."

"Can I read your book?" I asked. "Before I commit to anything?"

"No," Beals responded sharply, almost before I'd finished asking the question. "It's still being edited."

I was becoming irritated with his attitude. I didn't ask to be involved. It was his publisher who asked me to attend this meeting.

"That might make knowing what I am expected to photograph difficult. Reading what you have written would help, wouldn't you agree?"

"I will do what I can to get you a copy before you leave," Ernestine interjected, frowning at Beals. Turning back to me, she pressed, "So—what do you think?"

On the one hand, the opportunity held an undeniable allure. Except for the time on the boat, my recent travels to the South Pacific had been an unparalleled adventure, rivaled only by my days spent roaming Paris. Traveling to another tropical island while chasing down the secrets of a tyrannical despot was the stuff of pulp novels.

On the other hand: "Exactly how dangerous will it be?" I asked, unable to keep the tinge of wariness from creeping into my voice.

The dimly lit, smoke-wreathed interior of Sardi's seemed to grow darker as Beals leaned forward dramatically. His voice thick with emotion, he said, "In September, I arranged to meet Clemente Bello, President of the Senate, at the Havana Yacht Club. The next day, he was murdered getting in his car.

"That afternoon, I was to see Leopoldo Freyre de Andrade, an authority on the sugarcane disaster caused by Machado's policies and supported by Ambassador Guggenheim and the State Department." A muscle jumped in the hinge of Beals's jaw as he paused, worrying at his lower lip. "He didn't show, and I learned he and his two brothers were dead.

"Later the same day," Beals recounted as if reading from a police report, "Machado's band of murderers mowed down Congressman Aquiar as he came out of his house. He was on his way to meet me."

I stared at Beals in horror, imagining the echo of shattering glass and the acrid stench of gunpowder hanging in the air. The small amount of interest I had a moment before evaporated. What the hell were they thinking? Did they actually propose I enter a blood bath like that?

Ernestine cleared her throat, attempting to defuse the tension Beals was purposely creating. "Carleton, dear, I think you're scaring the boy." Throwing me an indulgent wink, she continued. "It's not as bad as all that, Walker. If you have read any of Carleton's works, you know he wields a pen dipped in hot blood. No one will ever accuse him of writing tepid prose. It is what has made him so popular—and effective. Unfortunately, he talks the way he writes."

"Look here, old man," Beals said in a calmer voice, though his eyes still smoldered, "I won't attempt to sugarcoat it. Cuba is an exceedingly dangerous place, but I wasn't in any real danger, personally." He chuckled self-consciously at the absurdity of his own statement before continuing. "The men Machado had murdered were slated for death whether I met with them or not. Luckily, we were not together when it happened."

"I'm not sure this is for me," I confessed. "Do you really need photographs in the book, or—"

"No," Beals said firmly, cutting me off. "The book stands on its own."

"Carleton," Ernestine said as if she were speaking to a child, "we've been over this. Walter agrees. If Walker comes back with a meaningful representation of Cuban life and what is happening now, if he compliments your writing, we will incorporate them into the book."

Her statement was clearly the last word on the subject. Beals did well not to pout.

She faced me directly. "You, Walker, will make more money than you have ever seen. You will receive a full five percent of the royalties. We'll feature your most striking image on the dust jacket—your name will be prominently displayed alongside Carleton's on the interior title page, with a biographical blurb on the back cover."

She leaned over the table, taking my hand in hers. "This book will be a sensation, my dear. It will make you famous."

And just like that—against all prudence, against all instinct for self-preservation—I was in.

Two

IT TOOK TWELVE DAYS to arrange the trip. I saw Beals twice more while I waited for Ernestine to purchase my ticket and make hotel reservations.

Our first encounter after the lunch at Sardi's was at a long, raucous party at his place on the Upper West Side. I was pleased to receive an invitation, but we never spoke other than a greeting at the door.

The party began at four and continued well past midnight. I got cornered by a very intoxicated Dash Hammett, who had recently finished his fifth novel, a story about a detective and his socialite wife. MGM, he bragged, had already optioned it for a film starring William Powell and Myrna Loy. Eventually, I was saved by Lily Hellman, who insisted he eat something.

My friend Diego was there with his bewitching wife, Frida Kahlo. She was still adjusting to New York after their time in Detroit and fuming over a recent article claiming that, as the wife of a great artist, she "gleefully dabbles in works of art." The more she drank, the fiery she became, rebuffing Diego's attempts to placate her. I was completely smitten.

The second meeting with Beals was another lunch with Ernestine.

During this encounter, Beals talked more about his book and his passion for exposing the deceit and corruption in the United States' involvement in Central America and the Caribbean. He stated several times that our country needed to support democracy or stay the hell out.

I learned that *The Crime of Cuba*, his sixth book, was more than an indictment of American Imperialism; it was also a chronicle of the island's tumultuous history and the diversity of its inhabitants. Above all, it was a plea for justice for a nation deserving far better than it had ever received.

The only disagreement came when I insisted on having the final say in selecting the photographs for his book and the order in which they would appear. Beals said no, the choice was his, and Ernestine frowned, silently voicing her dissent. Yet, with a diplomat's grace, she assured me she would endeavor to find a resolution.

As we parted for the last time, Beals handed me a list of several journalists in Havana, men who would aid my mission. Most important among them was my primary contact—José

Fernández de Castro Garrido,[5] a journalist for the influential *Diario de la Marina* and an outspoken critic of the Machado regime.

"Find José," Beals had said, "and no harm will come to you." Then he leveled his gaze at me and spoke in a serious tone. "However, there is one man in particular I recommend you avoid. His name is Colonel Jiménez, head of Machado's Secret Police. Don't get mixed up with him."

I assured Beals I had no intention of getting involved with any of Machado's men.

He also suggested I look as much like a tourist as I could. "You will be watched," he said, walking away.

So, heeding his advice, I bought a new lightweight tropical suit, sporty round sunglasses, and a straw boater. Still, I doubted a man carrying an unwieldy view camera and tripod on his shoulder would ever be completely camouflaged by white linen.

And it didn't take long for Beals's warning to come true.

On the chill, rainy afternoon, as I waited to present my ticket and board the SS *Virginia*, I had a strange feeling of being watched. I climbed the slippery gangway to the main deck and found a

---

[5] José de Castro, called by his father's surname, is a fictional amalgam of several journalists with whom Walker Evans interfaced in Cuba.

covered spot at the railing. There wasn't much of a crowd on the pier to wish us a *bon voyage*, so two shadowy figures caught my attention.

Dressed in dark brown suits, their faces partially concealed beneath wide-brimmed fedoras, they stared intently in my direction. For a moment, our eyes locked. Then, apparently realizing I had spotted them, they dipped their heads and walked off the pier, quickly disappearing in the rain.

Was I being paranoid? Why would anyone want to see me board a ship? At the time, I dismissed it as mere fancy, a fleeting figment of an overactive mind. Only later, in the shadows of Havana, would Beals's final words come back to haunt me.

Lippincott balked at my request for a first-class ticket, as I had expected. Instead, I found myself confined to a cramped tourist cabin on D Deck furnished with a single cot, a meager wash basin, and a locked portal. However, I was pleased it was a single room and didn't have to share the space.

Across the narrow passageway were the heads, as I knew to call them, housing toilet stalls and bathtubs. The ticket price of $135 included three meals and an endless supply of alcohol. I managed to secure an upgrade for an additional $10, granting me access to the opulent first-class dining room, bar, and promenade deck. From the conversation I overheard among my fellow tourists, the upgrade was worth the extra expense.

Virginia, a splendid vessel, was only four years old. Constructed in Newport News, Virginia, the ship stretched an impressive 613 feet in length and 80 feet in width, making her perfectly suited for navigating the Panama Canal. *Virginia* commanded respect on the high seas with a cruising speed of seventeen knots.

On this voyage, all the cabins were occupied. Among the passengers were 385 in first class and 365 tourists, accompanied by a crew of 350. You would never know the world was in the midst of a Depression based on the number of people traveling for enjoyment.

The crowded ship was a far cry from the luxurious 170-foot schooner I had sailed on during my South Seas adventure the previous year. On that boat, I could always find a secluded corner on deck to lose myself in a book from the well-stocked library. In contrast, with over a thousand souls aboard *Virginia*, the search for solitude proved difficult.

Most passengers were bound for the West Coast, sixteen days away, but many, like myself, would go no farther than Cuba. They all intended to take advantage of the one great benefit of traveling by ship—the fact that we were outside US jurisdiction and beyond the reach of the Volstead Act. Real alcohol, not just the recently unrestricted beer and wine, flowed like the water beneath our bow.

It soon became evident that the SS *Virginia* had a great deal of liquor on board. We departed Pier 16 in the early evening of May 16th. By 9 p.m., half the passengers, tourists and first-class alike, were lost in a blur of drunkenness. They remained in that state for the entire two-and-a-half-day voyage to Havana. Empty bottles cascaded overboard, leaving a trail of 'dead marines' to mark our passing.

After dinner on the first evening, I found my way to the first-class smoking lounge—a richly appointed room with knotty pine paneling on the walls and ceiling that evoked images of an exclusive Upstate hunting lodge. Dimly lit by wall-mounted lights designed to resemble antique oil lamps, the room boasted small tables and plush leather armchairs.

The satisfying scent of cigar smoke hung thick in the air as I found an empty table with a comfortable high-backed chair and immersed myself in the pages of *Ulysses*, a book I was pleased to discover in the ship's library. Much had changed in the world since the first publication of this controversial work a decade earlier.

Engaged as I was in re-discovering the trials and tribulations of Stephen Dedalus, I failed to notice the man standing next to my chair until he spoke.

"Never appreciated it, myself," a smoothly modulated voice said, interrupting my thoughts.

Surprised by his sudden appearance, I dropped the massive book on the floor.

"Dear me," the man apologized as he stooped to pick it up, "I didn't mean to startle you, Mr. Evans."

"No, no," I stammered. "You're fine. My mind was elsewhere."

"May I join you?" the man inquired, gesturing at the empty chair with a wave of his hand.

Mentally sighing, I reluctantly accepted the prospect of company and conversation. "Please," I responded cheerfully, straightening in my chair.

The man, older than me but undoubtedly younger than he looked, was tall and balding, possessing a prominent forehead, thick eyebrows, and piercing blue eyes. A thin lampshade mustache complimented his upper lip. His impeccable dark gray suit hung flawlessly on his slender frame.

He settled into the opposite chair, crossed his legs, and adjusted his trouser seam. Extending his hand, he said, "Sumner Welles."[6]

I knew Sumner Welles was FDR's newly appointed Ambassador to Cuba. His voice exuded refinement and sophistication, a product of his upbringing and unique diplomatic career. I recognized him from the recent newspaper articles that detailed his daunting task of replacing Ambassador Guggenheim and attempting to bring the warring factions in Cuba to the negotiation table, thereby ending the reign of terror documented by Beals.

Leaning forward to shake his hand, I began to introduce myself when I realized he already knew my name. The revelation sent a jolt coursing through me. Why would someone in Welles's position be aware of me?

"Ambassador," I said, my voice steady but my composure shaken, "it's an honor. Your appointment has been the talk of the town. My congratulations."

Welles dipped his chin in acknowledgment. For a moment, he studied me, eyes locked on my

---

[6] Benjamin Sumner Welles (1892—1961) was a major foreign policy adviser to President Franklin D. Roosevelt. In May, 1933 he was appointed the President's special envoy to Cuba with the official title of Ambassador Extraordinary and Plenipotentiary. He later served as Under Secretary of State from 1936 to 1943, when he lost his job due to rumors of homosexuality.

face, his perfectly manicured fingers intertwined on his crossed legs. Finally, he said, "You, Mr. Evans, are embarking on a convoluted and dark road." A slight smile played on his thin lips.

"I beg your pardon?" I said, licking my dry lips. Beals's parting words came to me: *"You will be watched."*

Welles nodded toward the book resting on the table between us. "Joyce," he said evenly. "It is not an easy read nor a light one. I recall it being rather dark. Do you not find it so?"

Taking a slow breath, I gathered my thoughts and composed myself. "I read it many years ago," I answered, trying to sound nonchalant. "During my time in Paris."

"Ah," Welles said, his tone smooth and calculated. "The perfect place to discover Joyce, I must admit. So many interesting people in one city at one time. Joyce lived there, I believe."

"Yes. As a matter of fact, I met him once," I offered, trying to regain some ground in the conversation.

Welles was intrigued. He raised one eyebrow. "Indeed, how did it come about, if I may ask?"

"I got to know Sylvia Beach quite well," I replied, name-dropping the Shakespeare and Company bookstore owner. "I met her in '26 while I was at school in Paris."

"A wonderful time to be in Paris," Welles interjected warmly. "And that's where you met Joyce?"

Welles's diplomatic charm was disarming. Yet, amidst the exchange, I couldn't help but wonder if there was more to Welles's interest in me. His enigmatic comment of a convoluted and dark road lingered in my mind, hinting at hidden secrets beneath his polished façade.

"I loved the bookstore," I continued, "and spent a great deal of time there. Joyce was often there as well. One day, Sylvia introduced us. I described my writing, my love of photography, all the reasons I had come to Paris."

"And what did he say to you?" Welles asked, his eyes fixed on mine.

I hesitated, wanting to tell Welles the truth about James Joyce, the impact the twentieth century's greatest writer had on me as a young man struggling with his art. Instead, I said, "He told me not to be a writer unless I could be a great writer; anything less is a waste of time."

Welles laughed loudly, his voice jarring in the large room. "I never met the man, although your description certainly fits my image of him." Rising from his seat, he extended his hand. "Well, I won't keep you from your book. It's been a pleasure, Mr. Evans. I hope to talk with you again."

Before Welles could leave, I had to ask: "Ambassador, how do you know who I am?"

A subtle tilt of his head accompanied Welles's response, his words carrying a threatening edge. "Walker Evans? Twenty-nine years old. Born in Chicago, raised in Ohio; father recently deceased. Now living in New York City with a friend. A promising photographer known for capturing the essence of the iconic Brooklyn Bridge. Who doesn't know Walker Evans?" Suddenly cold and menacing, his smile held a hidden depth as he added, "Goodnight, Mr. Evans."

With a graceful turn, Sumner Welles exited the smoking room, leaving me alone to grapple with the weight of his words and the meaning of our encounter. I knew one thing for certain—this journey to Cuba had become very real.

Ulysses went unread that night.

Three

HOW I HATE THE SEA.

Is anything more boring or mundane than an endless, flat, and featureless seascape? There is no form or shape. The sea, the clouds, and the waves blend and blur together in an unsettling and nauseating nothingness.

The creations of man, not the hand of God, stirs what soul I may possess. The rigid angles and unwavering lines of modern buildings, the towering slabs of concrete standing tall against the bitterly cold blue sky. A well-constructed vanishing point moves me more than an endless horizon ever could.

However, not all art needs sharp angles and hard edges. I can equally appreciate the gentle curve of a Victorian balustrade or the graceful catenary of a telephone line dipping in the summer heat.

The ocean holds no allure for me. I had enough of it in the South Pacific to last a lifetime.

Following Hart's death, I swore I would never be on the ocean again.

Yet, here I was.

To spare myself the torment, I spent my first full day at sea, avoiding the cold, monotonous vista. Fortunately, there were places on the ship that did not require staring at that endless horizon for hours as those poor souls buried in layers of blankets on their deck chairs did.

As the holder of an upgraded ticket, I had access to the library, the smoking room, the grand dining room, and the promenade deck. After a delightful chicken salad and double Gin Rickey lunch, I strolled onto the pool deck, where several fools braved the chilly water. The steward offered me a towel, assuring me the pool was heated to a balmy seventy degrees. I declined and found a deck chair out of the cool breeze and tried to lose myself in my book.

I tried, but my mind would not settle enough to read. I couldn't stop thinking about my encounter with Sumner Welles the previous night. I was disturbed that he knew so many personal details. Carleton Beals was well known to the State Department, and it seemed I had become a subject of their surveillance by association.

A cold gust prompted me to abandon the pool deck and seek the library's warmth. On the promenade deck, I passed groups of passengers happily engaged in shuffleboard, quoits, and deck tennis, though the ship's movement definitely affected the accuracy of the latter two. Others reclined on the deck lounge chairs, entombed in layers of blankets and scarves. I avoided looking out to sea as I moved forward, eventually finding a corner to myself in the library.

I opened *Ulysses*, found my page, and placed it gently on my chest. Exhausted by the weight of my thoughts, I fell into a restless sleep, dreaming of evil men lurking in the shadows of Havana.

The moon rose early, our second evening on the ocean. According to the captain's presentation at dinner, the ship was off the Carolinas and making good time. He anticipated a voyage of fifty-seven hours, which I found exceedingly brash. How could anyone possibly calculate that level of accuracy?

I sat at a table with a group of four other single men. Three of the group were salesmen with a shoe company bound for a convention in San Francisco. After initial introductions, they talked shop among themselves. That left me doing everything I could to ignore the grade-school math teacher on his first solo vacation since losing his wife. Twice during the second course, he began to tear up as he described his thirty years of marriage to the most wonderful woman in the world.

I couldn't wait to escape the table and, in my desperation, went so far as to venture on deck. The wind had died down, and the half-moon was low on the horizon, creating a splash of cream on the rippling waters. Stars sparkled with a brightness unseen in the city. Even I had to admit it was a beautiful sight.

A whiff of cigar smoke blew past me, and I realized another person was on deck forward from where I stood. When I looked in his direction, a familiar voice said, "Mr. Evans, how nice to see you again. Enjoying the evening air?"

Sumner Welles emerged from the dark shadows cast by the yellow deck lights. Once again, he was impeccably dressed in grey slacks, a blue blazer, and a crimson Harvard tie. Evidently, the man did not travel light.

"Good evening, Ambassador," I said while seeking a polite way to escape.

Welles reached inside his jacket and withdrew another cigar. "May I interest you in an excellent Havana? *Romeo y Julieta*, compliments of the Captain."

"No, thank you," I said. "I never acquired the taste." I tapped out one of my Chesterfields and attempted to light it. The wind was too strong for the paper match.

Welles chuckled. "Allow me," he said, scratching a wooden match on the railing. I leaned in to catch the flame, and he placed his hand against mine, lingering slightly longer than necessary to steady the match. "My wife does not approve," he said after we both had a drag on our respective tobaccos. "She detests the smell and makes me go out on the porch—or on deck, in this case."

I enjoyed the smell of a cigar even though my stomach did not. We stood together, silently smoking, watching the ocean pass. It was remarkably tranquil.

Then Welles said, "So what takes you to Cuba, Mr. Evans? If you don't mind my asking." His tone indicated he didn't care if I minded or not.

Unsure why he wanted to play this cat-and-mouse game, I decided to be just as coy. "What makes you think I am not headed for San Francisco?"

Welles blew a cloud of smoke and smiled at me in a most patronizing way. "Come, Mr. Evans, we all know where you are going. The question everyone is asking is—why? I am very much aware of Mr. Beals's visit last year, and I know he is writing a critical book on President Machado's regime. What I don't understand is why Lippincott has sent you. Your expertise is photography, I know, but I would have thought it a bit late to illustrate Mr. Beals's book. Isn't it scheduled for publication soon? Seem like a waste of money to me."

"I wouldn't know any publication plans," I said. Clearly, Welles knew more than he was saying, and my father always believed that a small amount of truth is better than a lie. "I've been hired to take photos of Cuba and Cubans, not Machado. I don't know what is in Beals's book," I added truthfully.

"Humpf," Welles grunted.

Before I could excuse myself and slip away, he said, "Tell me, Mr. Evans, what do you make of the situation in Cuba?"

"I'm sure I wouldn't know. I've never been there."

Welles exhaled slowly, examined his cigar stub, and fired it into the sea. He turned his back to the ocean and leaned against the railing. "Cuba is a child, Mr. Evans. A child needing guidance and a firm hand. Until the Spanish-American War, Spain provided that hand, if not the necessary guidance. They ruled the island for one purpose—profit. They cared little for the island and less for its people. While we may have mismanaged the war, the end result was what we, the United States, wanted: After four hundred years, Spain lost its foothold in this hemisphere, and the United States gained valuable land assets around the world."

"So, Cuba was the excuse for our imperialism," I said, emboldened by the man's posturing. "It has been thirty-five years since we defeated Spain. Has Cuba improved under our parenting?"

"Have you ever heard of the Platt Amendment?" Welles asked. His head was backlit by the deck light, which made his face inscrutable.

"Can't say I have," I answered stiffly. I felt like a pupil forced to listen to the teacher's lecture.

"As I said, Cuba is like a child. In this case, a child caught in a bitter divorce. Until we defeated Spain, Cuba had no say in her own destiny. After the war she was without guidance, floundering in the new world order. We stepped in and assumed the parental role Spain had so mismanaged. The Platt Amendment was incorporated into the new Cuban constitution, giving the United States oversight of the poor, fledgling country. Of utmost importance is the part prohibiting Cuba from engaging in any treaty or change in government that does not support democracy in the country. I am going to Cuba to ensure President Machado adheres to that agreement before we are forced to take action."

"So," I ventured, "you aren't supporting Machado's regime, *per se*. Your interest is in assuring democracy, no matter who is in charge. Is that it?"

Welles tilted his head instead of shrugging his shoulders. "We would prefer President Machado stays in power."

"I've read that Machado was a nationalist who vowed to defend the workers and uproot the monopolies the United States has established in Cuba."

"You do know something of Cuban politics," Welles said. "Yes, Machado said that. It got him elected in 1925. He may been serious in the beginning, although it didn't last. He always had ties with the US that he never intended to sever. Ties, quite frankly, we don't want to jeopardize. However, Machado announced he was arbitrarily extending his tenure as president. The decision has ignited an unstoppable conflagration of protests, strikes, and outrage from all sectors of Cuban society."

"Then the problem," I said with a flash of insight, "is that you've lost control of him. And you can't allow the disruption to continue. Machado has become a liability. That's the real issue, isn't it?"

This time, Welles did shrug. "No," he said, pushing away from the rail, "that's not the issue. The issue is the Cuban people no longer live in a democracy, something that is of critical importance to us."

I snorted at his blatant guile. "Uh-huh. Platt Amendment aside, what gives us the right to intervene in Cuban politics anyway? They elected Machado. Is it not their problem to solve?"

"No, Mr. Evans. The child needs a parent's steadying hand. And will for many years to come." He held out his own hand. "Do take care in Cuba, Mr. Evans. There are undercurrents you are not prepared to navigate. Good night."

With that chilling parting remark, Welles was once more swallowed by the shadows. I stood for a time as the moon rose in the starry sky until the chill air drove me below deck to my cramped cabin.

I didn't see Sumner Welles again until the SS *Virginia* docked in Havana thirty-six hours later.

Four

THE BLINDING WHITE LIGHT reflected off the concrete, the dark green water, and the windshields of two large black sedans waiting on the pier.

I donned my new sunglasses and pulled the brim of the boater lower over my forehead. Despite the heat and dampness spoiling my collar, I felt rather dapper, dressed in the cream-colored linen suit purchased for the trip. Suddenly, I also felt very exposed.

Some other passengers lining up to show their passports to the Cuban immigration officer were also dressed in their tropical best. Those in heavier cloth were going ashore for the half day *Virginia* would spend in Havana before continuing to Panama and San Francisco.

As I shuffled forward, the Star Spangled Banner echoed against the side of the ship. I looked over the railing in time to see Ambassador Welles and his wife descending the gangway. An officer in the US Marines, a small Marine band, and a Cuban dignitary waited for them at the bottom of the steep ramp. After handshakes and salutes, and a bouquet of flowers for Mrs. Welles, the party entered the waiting limos. The two motorcycle escorts started their machines, and the parade roared up the pier and into the city. The Marines marched after them.

Finally, it was my turn to face the immigration officer sitting at a small folding table. The man was dark complected with a full mustache and dressed in a nondescript military uniform, cap, and sunglasses. He took my passport as if already suspecting me of an unknown crime.

Between the early morning heat and humidity, the press of bodies, and the scrutiny of the officer, sweat trickled down my temple, betraying my nerves.

It did not go unnoticed by the officer.

Looking from my passport photo to me, he pointed at my sunglasses and barked, "*¡Quitate las gafas!*"

I understood the command, if not the words, and removed my sunglasses, allowing him to scrutinize my face more closely. His forehead furrowed in concentration as if searching for something.

"You are Señor Walker Evans?" he questioned in accented but precise English.

"Yes…" I replied and cleared my throat. "Yes."

"What is your business in Cuba?" he continued in a challenging tone.

Clearing my throat again, I responded cautiously, "I'm here as a tourist. I always wanted to see—"

"Show me your return ticket," he interrupted.

I removed the ticket from my billfold and handed it to the officer. He studied it closely, his eyes darting from the ticket to my face. After a moment, he returned the ticket and motioned me to proceed to the next official.

Joining the line of disembarking passengers, I made my way to the table where our luggage was inspected. The officer's eyes lingered on my camera equipment, suspicion clouding his face. Then, he waved his hand dismissively, allowing me to proceed.

Balancing my suitcase and camera, I descended the gangway and entered Cuba.

Walking down the pier to Desamparados Street was like stepping back in time. Except for the multitude of vehicles belching clouds of exhaust, nothing resembled the 20th century I had left behind in New York City.

Vying for a place on the wide boulevard were large wheeled vegetable carts pulled by emaciated donkeys, young boys hocking colorful packs of candy and fruit, carriage drivers outshouting each other for the attention of the disembarking tourists, and a couple of lovely ladies lounging in the shade of the arches.

The cacophony of noise and pungent odors assailed my senses from all directions.

I later realized my taxi driver had taken me on a circuitous tour of Havana before stopping at the Hotel Florida, only five blocks from where we had started. He asked for ten pesos, and I gave him a dollar. He went away happy.

The Hotel Florida was a magnificent structure, exceeding all my expectations. Its towering, beige sandstone columns framed the open central atrium, supporting a wrap-around balcony on the third floor. The wide arches and black and white tiles lent the place an exotic Moroccan ambiance. The glass skylight high overhead bathed the lobby in a cool, ethereal glow.

I was stunned that Lippincott would indulge in such luxury.

My room on the top floor at the rear of the building offered respite from the commotion on Calle Obispo, one of Havana's busiest shopping streets. I could see the edge of a small, tranquil park lined with trees through the gracious open window. It seemed like an oasis amidst the bustling, dusty city and a sanctuary from the prying eyes I suspected followed my every move.

However, my journey to the quiet fifth floor had its challenges. The temperamental elevator often left me stranded, forcing me to climb the stairs, a feat that sapped the last remnants of my energy after a long day in the city. Fortunately, the times it worked outnumbered the days a sign read: ¡*No Servicio!*

Stretching out on the single bed, I intended to take a short nap, waiting for the cool breeze to re-energize me before setting out to find my contact. Instead, I fell into a fitful sleep and didn't rise until 2 p.m.

Hungry and disoriented from my nap, I found the hotel restaurant for a late lunch. A plate of pulled pork, black beans, yellow rice, and a side order of fried plantains satisfied my hunger. I washed it down with two room-temperature *la Tropicals*, hoping to shake off the thick-headed feeling. Then, I exchanged most of Ernestine's cash advance into peso bills and a handful of unidentifiable coins. I placed half in my billfold and deposited the rest in the hotel safe.

The primary person on Beals's contact list was José Fernández de Castro Garrido, a journalist with *Diario de la Marina*, the conservative, anti-Machado newspaper. Beals had explained that Cubans continued the Spanish tradition of using their father's surname followed by their mother's. De Castro used his father's name as his byline, and most people knew him by that name.

The hotel desk clerk informed me that newspaper offices closed at noon on Fridays and would reopen in the morning. It was still relatively early, so I showed the clerk de Castro's address, and he explained how to find it in notable detail.

Feeling conspicuous, I waited with half a dozen questionable men at the bus stop as open-air buses came and went. Soon, I noticed a man who seemed particularly interested in my presence. Each time our eyes met, he averted his.

As each bus, which the desk clerk inexplicably called a *wawa*, screeched to a stop, I would approach the entrance and, in my best Spanish, ask, "*¿Santos Suarez?*"

Eventually, one driver replied in the affirmative, and I attempted to board the bus. My billfold contained large peso notes, and the driver refused to make change. Somewhat flustered, I searched all my pockets for the coins I had received at the hotel. I held a handful out to the driver, unsure of the cost of the bus ride. He took them all.

With a curt nod toward an empty seat, the bus lurched forward, bouncing and swaying on the cobblestone streets. By now, I was perspiring heavily, so I folded my suit jacket, laid it across the seat, and tried to relax for the thirty-minute ride to the suburb of Santos Suarez.

As we rumbled along, I surreptitiously examined each person, wishing I had my reflex camera with its ninety-degree lens. I have often obtained candid shots of unsuspecting people with that lens. I resolved to never venture out without it again.

And what a collection of suspicious characters it was. In addition to the man who had watched me at the bus stop, I caught other passengers peering at me from the corner of their eyes. I was convinced that two men dressed in dark suits and large-brimmed fedoras worked for Machado. They exuded an air of authority far different than a regular commuter. Were they part of the murder squad Beals had mentioned? Men assigned to silence anyone who dug too deep? How many more were lurking in the shadows?

The view of the city changed as we drove away from Old Havana. Ancient, crumbling buildings gave way to newer, single-story structures. After an interminable amount of time, the bus rocked to a stop on a steep street. The bus driver looked over his shoulder at me, a wide grin on his face, and bellowed, "¡*Esto es Santos Suarez!*"

I rose from my seat, gathered my jacket, and began to move to the exit. A man grabbed my arm, halting me in my tracks. At first, I feared the hand belonged to one of Machado's spies. To my surprise, the man pointed to the seat I had vacated.

There, on the worn and cracked seat, lay my billfold.

A surge of relief washed over me as I hastily retrieved it and thanked the man in Spanish. I descended to the deserted street. The bus belched a cloud of black smoke and roared away, leaving me alone on the road, clutching my jacket in one hand and billfold in the other. I donned my jacket and checked the billfold before inserting it into my breast pocket. A chilling realization made my heart stand still.

All of my cash had vanished.

I had been robbed!

Frantically, I patted the other pockets of my suit. Nothing. Someone had picked my billfold from my jacket and left it on the seat.

Anger mingled with a sense of shame engulfed me in a storm of emotions. What a way to start my Cuban adventure. Robbed! In broad daylight on a public bus. I almost stomped my foot in frustration. Then, a more relevant thought entered my mind: how would I pay for the bus ride back to the hotel?

I desperately surveyed my surroundings with unease creeping up my spine. Single homes crowded together on the narrow street with water flowing freely in the gutter. I would have expected de Castro to live in a more affluent part of the city. This type of housing did not fit the impression of the journalist I had gotten from Beals. I opened the paper on which I had written his address and the instructions provided by the hotel clerk.

According to the clerk, I had to walk three blocks farther up the hill. José de Castro's house would be the second one on the right. Bitterly angry with myself, I trudged onward.

The address on my note led me to a two-story blue stuccoed house wedged between two taller buildings. Its wooden front door was protected by a wrought iron grating. I reached between the rusting rods and banged on the door.

Silence echoed from within. Next door, a dog barked.

Growing more frustrated and desperate, I pounded on the door again. What a disastrous trip this was turning into. I should have waited to find José at his office tomorrow. Coming here was an ill-conceived plan.

As I was about to leave, a man opened the door of the neighboring house. He wore black trousers and a filthy wife-beater undershirt, a machete gripped tightly in his hand, and a cigar stub in his teeth. A menacing, non-descript dog growled by his side.

"*¿Que estas haciendo aquí?*" he shouted. Though I didn't understand the words, the hostility in his voice was clear.

"Señor de Castro?" I asked, pointing at the door I had been attacking.

The man squinted at me, his gaze filled with suspicion, before replying, "*El no está aquí,*" and slammed his door shut.

Now what, I asked myself.

The sun was low on the horizon, creating long shadows in the street. Beyond the city, dark rain clouds loomed over the ocean. A good soaking would be a fitting addition to my predicament.

Feeling sorry for myself and despising my stupidity in this venture, I started back down the hill to the bus stop. I had only gone a hundred yards when a car appeared on the street behind me. The glare of its headlights made me shade my eyes, a movement the driver interpreted as a request to stop. Miracle upon miracle, the sedan's door displayed the words *Golden Taxi* in yellow block letters.

"Are you lost?" a voice asked in lightly accented English.

Caught off guard, I stammered, "I, I don't have any money for the bus back to town. Can you help me? I need to get to my hotel."

The driver, a young man with slicked-back hair and a cigarette between his fingers, grinned at me through a cloud of smoke.

"No American should take the bus in Cuba. Can you pay your fare when you get to your hotel?" he asked.

Nodding like an idiot, I said, "Yes, yes, I can!" and wearily settled into the backseat, my exhaustion overwhelming me.

I must have dozed off, for the next thing I knew, the car had stopped in front of the Hotel Florida. I told the driver to wait while I recovered my money from the front desk.

With a wave of thanks, the driver gunned the engine and sped away. Lost in thought, I watched the car race down the dark street and turn the corner.

It was a remarkably fortunate accident that he came along when he did, or I would have had a long walk back to the Hotel Florida…

Only then did I realize *I had never told the driver the name of my hotel.*

Five

I WOKE LATE, still exhausted from the previous day's activities. Determined to make today count, I stumbled into the hotel restaurant and ordered a strong *café con leche* to clear the cobwebs. There is nothing like Cuban coffee to jump-start the senses.

Hailing a taxi at the corner, I directed the driver to take me to the office of the *Diario de la Marina*. As we weaved through the narrow streets, I noted that most shops, many with English signs, were closed.

"The shops," I queried the driver in broken Spanish, *"cerrada. Por que?"*

He answered without taking his eyes off the crowded street, *"¡Dia de la Independencia!"*

I leaned back, craning my neck to admire the intricate carvings and elaborate ornaments adorning the building facades. The architecture of Havana is a stunning mixture of imperial, Baroque, and neo-classical, all crammed together on streets so narrow that traffic must flow in one direction. On each side, equally narrow sidewalks, often obstructed by parked cars, force pedestrians to maneuver past each other.

At a distance, the graceful columns, ornate pediments, and church towers reaching for the heavens represented monuments to Spain's extravagant lifestyle. But, as some poor pedestrians learned daily, the buildings were literally falling apart. Especially after a hard rain, chunks of stucco or carved stone littered the streets.

At the end of Teniente Rey Street, directly across the Paseo de Marti, the neo-classical white dome of the capitol building loomed high over the city. It truly was a spectacular structure. Constructed four years earlier, Machado had shamelessly copied the design of the US Capitol and insisted on making his dome thirteen feet higher.

The driver stopped next to a corner building flanked by high arches opening to a covered sidewalk. This design, found everywhere in Old Havana, allowed pedestrians to walk in the shade or protected from the tropical downpours.

A young boy at the front desk waved lethargically toward the center of the long, dimly lit room. The sun's rays filtered through drawn blinds, casting a brownish hue that complimented the scent of ink, old paper, and cigars permeating the air. Rows of desks lined a central corridor, most of them empty.

The desk indicated by the boy was occupied by a man in his mid-thirties with dark curly hair and a pencil-thin mustache above his full lips. Looking up from his work, an open and friendly smile spread across his face, revealing strong white teeth.

"Señor de Castro?" I asked.

He tilted his head, trying to grasp why I stood before him. "*¿Sí?*" Then, in strongly accented English, he continued, "May I help you?"

"Señor de Castro, my name is Walker Evans…" I began.

The smile faltered slightly. He obviously had no idea who I was. I removed Beals's letter from my breast pocket, unfolded it, and handed him the paper.

He accepted it silently, his eyes scanning the contents. "Ah, you are sent by Señor Beals! Such a wonderful man! So serious! Yes, I did not expect you until Monday. No matter! We will go to lunch, and we will talk! You will call me José. *¡Esta bien!* We go."

With that, he rose from his seat, snatching his jacket and Panama from the back of the chair. As we passed the front desk, he muttered something to the boy, who seemed indifferent to our departure. Stepping onto the street, the blinding sunlight assaulted my senses, and I fumbled for my sunglasses.

"First," he said, steering me by the elbow, "I must make a quick stop." We stepped to the curb, and a black and maroon Dodge four-door sedan materialized before us. De Castro and I climbed into the back. At first, I assumed it was a taxi, though I hadn't seen him hail one. Then I noticed another man sitting in the passenger seat, his broad shoulders and bald head accentuating the rolls of flesh on his thick neck. De Castro made no effort to introduce either the driver or this man.

Was he a bodyguard, I wondered. He certainly looked like he could handle any problem we encountered.

The car lurched forward and merged into the heavy traffic. While the driver deftly avoided cars and pedestrians intent on crossing the street in every direction, de Castro provided a running commentary.

"Twenty million US dollars! Can you believe that!" he grumbled, indicating the Capitol. "What this country could do with twenty million dollars."

We veered down a shadowy, deserted side street, stopping in front of an old storefront. Its exterior was dark with grime, the windows streaked inside and out. It did not appear to be occupied.

"I will be only one minute," de Castro said as he slammed the car door. "You will wait."

The driver and the bodyguard seemed content to follow his orders, so I sat back and waited.

I admit I felt a bit drunk. This city was so new and so much different from anything I had experienced. Paris was languid and sedate. Everything moved at a well-established pace. Havana, by comparison, had the feeling of a Wild West town, teetering on the edge of violence.

And what of this man, José de Castro?

Without Beals's letter of introduction, I would be slightly concerned for my well-being. De Castro seemed somewhat mad, a man who lived in the moment. He hadn't asked any questions, not even to inquire if I had other plans, as he whisked me out of his office building.

Yet, despite the uncertainty, I felt safe. I believed he was an honest and trustworthy man. Just overly enthusiastic, perhaps.

The door flew open, and de Castro crashed onto the seat beside me. "*¡Esta bien!* We go eat!" he announced.

Since it was already past noon, lunch was a quick sandwich and a lukewarm Hatuey at an outdoor cantina. Despite the temperature, I had to admit that the beer brewed locally by Bacardi was as good as their rum. The sandwich, stuffed with ham, pork, cheese, and pickles in a toasted bun, was equally tasty.

There were no chairs, so we stood in the cool shadows of the ubiquitous arches. I avoided leaning against the filthy stonework, overly conscious of my off-white suit.

As we ate, I took advantage of de Castro's momentary silence to tell him Beals sent his regards and thanks for helping me with my assignment. I explained my goal of capturing the true essence of Cuba.

"Señor Beals, he knows the real Cuba," de Castro observed. "Can your pictures add to what he writes?"

I chewed for a moment before answering as diplomatically as I could. "I hope my photos will compliment Mr. Beals's book while presenting my observations of Cuba in my own way."

"Ah," de Castro said, crumpling his wrapper and throwing it aside. "We go!"

Crossing to his waiting car, I mentioned my misadventure searching for his house.

"You were robbed?" he gasped, clutching his heart. "I have never heard of such an outrage!" I had to chuckle at De Castro's poor acting. "Did you lose all of your money?"

"No," I replied. "Half of it is in the hotel safe."

"I am not sure that is any better place to keep it." Then, lowering his sunglasses with one finger, he echoed the warning from the taxi driver, "Americans should not ride the bus in Cuba. We have a car. Do not take the bus again."

Confused by the maze of city streets, I discovered we were back at the *Diario de la Marina* office building. The scene was chaotic, with a crush of people filling the steps of the Capitol. I raised my voice to be heard over the clamor, "What's happening, José?"

"Come!" de Castro shouted. "We will get you a very good picture!"

Once inside the building, he walked to the dimly lit stairs and climbed the steps two at a time. We passed empty offices, rounded to the next stairs, and continued our climb. It got darker and darker as we ascended. De Castro abruptly banged against a steel door that opened onto the flat roof, putting us back in the glaring light, high above the crowded street.

"Here!" de Castro shouted, trotting to the parapet. I joined him more slowly, my stomach clenching. "We are just in time. The procession has not gone by."

"Procession?" I asked, steeling my nerve to peer over the edge. I have never been comfortable with heights, whether climbing a tree as a child or photographing the Brooklyn Bridge. To be honest, that's a gross understatement—I am terrified of heights and always have been. I wouldn't be caught dead in a tree.

But de Castro was correct. It was a great view of the Paseo de Marti and the capitol building. Farther north, toward the Malecón, the boulevard is tree-lined and perfect for an evening stroll. De Castro explained that Habaneros always referred to the street by its old name, Paseo del Prado.

The noise from the crowd below suddenly increased. I checked my camera settings, propping the Leica on the chest-high parapet. Below, four gleaming black Packards rounded the corner to our right, heading south. The predominantly male crowd cheered and waved their boaters in the air. I took several shots, zooming in as much as possible to capture the well-dressed men pushing and shoving to obtain a better view of their leader.

"Quickly!" de Castro shouted. "The motorcade will turn and pass us again. *El Presidente*, he is going to the statue of José Marti at the Parque Central. It is there." He pointed north, but a view of the park was blocked by the Payret Theatre.

Before I could comment, de Castro darted for the stairway, forcing me to follow or risk being stranded on the roof. Regaining the street, we joined the mass of humanity trailing the president's motorcade as it drove slowly toward the statue of Marti.

As we hurried along the crowded boulevard, de Castro continued his rapid-fire commentary.

"Marti and General Maximo Gomez, they are *los más grandes figuras* in our long and bloody fight for independence," de Castro huffed, his voice filled with national pride. "Marti was a *literatus* of global importance. He was a world-renowned poet, philosopher, and writer. Did you know he lived in the United States for some time? He raised money and spread the Cuban cause wherever he went. Alas, poor Marti, he was no soldier. He did not survive his first battle against the Spanish. Such a tragedy…"

De Castro clicked his tongue, momentarily lost in the memories of a fallen hero.

"Is this the independence being celebrated today?" I asked, matching de Castro stride for stride. "Marking Cuba's liberation from Spain?"

My guide shook his head adamantly. "No, no. We won our freedom from Spain in 1898 at the end of what you Americans call the Spanish-American War. Today, we celebrate our independence from the United States in 1902, when Cuba became a republic."

I thought back to the lesson Ambassador Welles taught me on the ship. The third Cuban War of Independence had raged from 1895 to 1898. The United States eventually joined the battle against Spain when the battleship *Maine* mysteriously exploded in Havana harbor.

The war marked the beginning of American Imperialism, a concept that Carleton Beals fiercely criticized. Spain was forced to relinquish Puerto Rico, the Philippines, and Guam to the United States, and American forces occupied Cuba until 1902. That was the day Cuba supposedly gained independence, albeit shackled by the provisions of the Platt Amendment.

"Four more years we endured your military occupation," de Castro continued, "and the indignity of having our future as a sovereign people dictated by the *norteamericanos*."

Recognizing the pain and emotion in his words, I did not reply and discreetly readied my camera as we pushed through the mass of people.

While many in the crowd cheered for their president, a larger number did not. The majority of spectators were subdued and sullen, as if they had been required to attend the festivities and would rather be elsewhere.

Tossed upon the sea of humanity, I found myself thrust to the front of the crowd. Ten feet from where I stood, a group of police wearing pristine white uniforms formed a half-circle around a solitary figure.

President Gerardo Machado [7], a man known for his charm as much as for his ruthless nature, stood tall and imperious. He wore round glasses like my sunglasses and a beautifully tailored charcoal grey suit. With his greying hair slicked back and his dark eyes scanning the crowd, the man projected an unmistakable aura of wealth and power.

I took three shots as the President placed a wreath at the foot of the gayly festooned statue of Marti, the Apostle of Freedom. Facing the crowd, he swiveled in my direction with predatory precision, and our eyes met. Those dark orbs bored into me—cold, unflinching, utterly devoid of warmth or humanity. Then, he noticed the camera in my hands and frowned.

Under different circumstances, one might mistake Machado for a sugar baron or shipping magnate. However, I knew better. Carleton Beals had described the true nature of this man. I was standing face-to-face with a vicious killer.

---

7 Gerardo Machado y Morales (1871—1939) was a general during the Cuban War of Independence and President of Cuba from 1925 to 1933. He died in Miami Beach, Florida.

Machado wagged his chin in my direction, and two uniformed shapes detached themselves from the cordon with military precision. My heart raced, knowing that I had become a target. I attempted to blend into the crowd, even though my light cream-colored suit and fair complexion made it impossible.

As the police closed in, shouts and cries of fear erupted from the crowd on the far side of the park.

A shot rang out.

A woman screamed.

The policemen instantly abandoned their interest in me and ran toward the commotion. Other officers manhandled Machado into his waiting limo.

Several men were being jostled by other police. One man, blood running from his forehead, lunged past an officer in an attempt to break free, only to be wrestled to the pavement. Another young man, dressed in a coat and tie, received a brutal blow to the jaw with the butt of a rifle.

The crowd surged away from the melee like the parting of the Red Sea. A strong hand grasped my elbow and pulled me into the masses.

"We go!" de Castro shouted in my ear, his voice urgent.

I didn't argue. We pushed across the Paseo Agromante and down a short street. The press of humanity cleared as we came to a small park. Doubled over, hands on our knees, we gasped for breath.

Only the absurd sound of de Castro's chuckling managed to rouse me.

"Welcome to *La Habana*, Señor Evans!"

I looked up, sweat dripping from my forehead. "What was that all about? An assassination attempt?"

He shrugged. "Perhaps, or students protesting against Machado. The ABC, maybe. Who knows? They did not plan it well and will be severely dealt with."

Then, indicating an open-air cantina opposite the park, he exclaimed, "*El Floridita!*" as if he had discovered Ponce de Leon's Fountain of Youth. "I believe it is time for a drink, do you not agree?"

I agreed wholeheartedly.

The conch-pink building was as disreputable as the restaurant where we had lunch. A neon sign hung above the corner entrance. Although early in the evening, the bar was crowded. Small tables and chairs spilled onto the narrow sidewalk. I spotted a few Americans, but most of the patrons were Cuban. Several attractive women loitered near the entrance. They smiled at us as we entered the bar.

We maneuvered to the long, worn bar occupying most of the interior space. Three bartenders worked feverishly, shaking silver cocktail mixers above their shoulders.

Within minutes, I held a pale concoction of slurry ice.

"What is this?" I asked, slowly sipping the sour drink.

De Castro leaned toward me, his voice low as if departing a state secret. "This drink, it was perfected by Constante, the owner and best bartender in Havana." He nodded toward one of the bartenders. "Some years ago, Constante created his version of the Daiquiri, which has become very popular. To make this drink, you take two ounces of Bacardi light rum and toss it in a shaker. Add one teaspoon of very fine sugar—not powdered. Then add one teaspoon of maraschino liqueur. Squeeze in the juice of half a lime, then a teaspoon of grapefruit juice. Toss in some cracked ice and shake very well."

Impressed by the detailed recipe, I couldn't help but ask, "You seem quite familiar with this drink. Have you had many?"

A wry smile played on de Castro's lips as he wagged his head from side to side. "Everyone in Havana loves the Daiquiri. There are several variations, but this is the one I like best. It is called Number 3." De Castro leaned closer. "But, however many you drink, it is never as many as that man sitting there."

I followed his gaze, nearly choking on my drink.

"You know who that is?" de Castro asked.

Indeed, I did. At the far corner of the bar, hunched over his frozen drink, sat Ernest Hemingway.

The literary icon was dressed in khaki shorts and a shirt rolled up to expose powerful, hairy arms. His dark, wavy hair was combed back, and a loose strand hung jauntily on his forehead. His trademark mustache had not been trimmed and hid his upper lip.

The man was plainly drunk, lost in his own alcoholic haze.

"Señor Hemingway is here each afternoon, usually by himself, and drinks Daiquiris until he is too drunk to drink. He keeps trying to break his own record."

"How many is that?"

"No one knows for sure. It depends on which bartender you ask." De Castro pushed away from the bar. "Come, I will introduce you."

Near panic swept over me. "No, no! It doesn't look like he's having a good time."

"Come! He will not bite!"

Not sure if that was true, I trailed de Castro to the end of the bar.

"Papa! ¿*Que pasa*?" de Castro said as he sat beside the writer. I stood by awkwardly, feeling exposed and out of place.

Hemingway raised his head and focused his bloodshot eyes on de Castro. "Go to hell, José."

Ignoring the slurred rebuke, de Castro said, "I wish to introduce a friend from America. This is Señor Evans. He is a photographer of great renown."

Hemingway turned blurry eyes in my direction. "Great renown, huh? Have I seen any of your work?"

"No," I admitted meekly, "Probably not."

Hemingway laughed gruffly, taking a sip from his Daiquiri. "Then fuck off," he said, dismissing my existence.

And that, after all these years, was how I finally met Ernest Hemingway [8].

---

[8] Ernest Miller Hemingway (July 21, 1899—July 2, 1961) first visited Havana in 1929. From 1932 to 1938, while living in Key West, he returned for frequent fishing trips, staying at the Hotel Ambos Mundos. Eventually, he made Cuba his permanent home, living at the Finca Vigia until 1960. Hemingway committed suicide in 1961.

Six

THANK GOD, the next day was Sunday. No sound intruded on my pounding head other than the church bells summoning the faithful and the occasional spat of gunfire in the distance, something I was becoming used to.

How many Daiquiris had we consumed? The evening was a blur. I know Hemingway staggered out of the bar hours before de Castro and I. How he manages that feat night after night is beyond me. De Castro thinks he is trying to kill himself.

Resolved to never drink again, I dressed in my grey gaberdine and fedora and once again found a taxi at the corner by the hotel. I asked the driver to take me to the Malecón.

The cabbie appeared to be in his eighties, spoke English, and was happy to describe the sites as he wound his way toward the waterfront and the Malecón. He pointed to the towering lighthouse and imposing walls of *Castillo de los Tres Reyes del Morro*, Havana's most iconic landmark. It was built, he said, in 1589 to protect the harbor from the English and Dutch marauders.

"And on this side," he continued, "are the ruins of *Castillo de San Salvador de la Punta*. Once, a huge chain of lumber stretched from *el Morro* to *la Punta*, making *La Habana* the most impenetrable harbor in the Americas."

The Malecón runs most of the length of Havana's waterfront. During the day, the road is teeming with noisy traffic. At night, the pace slows, and the breeze off the ocean is constant and refreshing after the heat and humidity of the day. Couples stroll arm in arm on the broad sidewalk or perch on the quay wall, lost in each other's embrace.

I paid the driver, refusing his offer to show me all of Havana. I took pictures of the fortress across the water and couples lounging on the quay wall. A strong wind created whitecaps in the bay and blew dust down the street, forcing me to jamb my hat onto my head while photographing.

After several hours of playing tourist and a light meal at the hotel, I turned in early that night. Tomorrow, I promised myself, I would find the type of dystopian images Ernestine expected. Decaying buildings, the poor waiting for food handouts, the police attacking protestors—I was sure de Castro would know where to find them.

However, he had a different agenda.

The next morning, de Castro picked me up in the same chauffeur-driven sedan. The bodyguard did not join us.

"You said you wished to get a view of all Havana," de Castro said with a malicious chuckle. "Knowing how much you love heights, I have something special for you. Photographs from a special vantage point will please your publisher. Perhaps they will be the only pictures ever taken from such a place. This building, it will be torn down soon."

Today, I brought my 6-1/2 x 8-1/2 view camera and tripod. I indicated the box sitting on the seat between us and said, "As long as you are willing to help carry the camera equipment. And, providing it's not too high…"

"Don't worry," de Castro laughed. "It is very high!"

Ten minutes later, we parked outside the fortress-like walls of the Plaza del Vapor. This massive building encompassed an entire block. The building was a three-story square wall surrounding a huge open space reminiscent of the old Spanish plazas.

The ground floor was crowded with small shops, clothing stores, fruit stalls, and dozens of other unidentifiable establishments. The upper floors housed hundreds of residents. These people are the lowest of Havana's poor. They lived in squalor, with laundry strung from balconies adorned with small flower pots.

After shooting different versions of the shops, de Castro pointed at the building on Dragones Street. Towering at least ten stories was the headquarters of the Cuban Telephone Company. I had to lean back to see the Baroque bell tower adorned with spires and lightning rods a hundred feet above the street.

"No, no, no," I said, grasping my camera box to my chest. "I am not going up there!"

De Castro took the camera from me. "Of course you are! You would not ignore such an opportunity. Besides, I have made special arrangements so that we may reach the very top. We go!"

I was pleased to see an electric lift in the lobby with a boy waiting patiently to take us to the tenth floor. The idea of climbing the stairs had made my knees weak. On the tenth floor, a door led to a spiral staircase. Already dizzy, I panted as we circled higher, finally emerging in the bell tower.

De Castro was right. The view nearly overcame my fear of heights. I tentatively approached the edge, careful not to look straight down to the street at least a thousand feet below. Or so it seemed.

The castle hovering over the green waters of the harbor and all of Old Havana were spread out before me. I set the camera on the tripod and prepared the plates.

Below, the enclosed area of del Vapor Plaza, paved in concrete and devoid of any trees or plants, was on full display. De Castro said it was large enough to play baseball. I exposed two more plates and packed the cameras.

On the top floor, the boy was waiting to return us to *Terra Firma*. My heart slowly returned to normal, and my knees regained their strength.

"We don't need to do that again," I said.

We stowed the bulky camera and tripod in the trunk, and I retrieved my trusty Leica from its case. Beneath a large arch, colorful racks of magazines and newspapers boxed in a shoeshine stand. A man perched on a high chair as a young boy vigorously buffed his shoes with practiced movements.

This was a scene I could not ignore. I discreetly snapped a few shots without anyone noticing my presence.

"We need to go," de Castro whispered urgently, his eyes darting toward a striking figure emerging from a large Packard sedan.

The man had a commanding presence. Tall and bone-thin, he wore a crisp, brilliantly white linen suit that contrasted sharply with his remarkably coal-black skin. A dark tie and a new boater completed the ensemble. His pockmarked, deeply-creased face exuded power and danger.

He crossed the street to the shoeshine stand with long, languid strides. Then, as he waited for an empty chair, unfathomable dark brown eyes surreptitiously scanned the area for any threat. A cigarette dangled between his delicate fingers, adding to the look of casual menace.

I quickly turned my back when the man in white glanced in my direction, but not before capturing a single shot.

"What are you doing!" de Castro hissed, his voice filled with alarm. "Do not take that man's picture! Come, we go!"

"Who is he?" I asked as we retreated to the safety of our vehicle.

De Castro did not answer until we were driving away. "That was Colonel Antonio Jiménez, head of the Secret Police and the man who runs *la Porra*."

"*Porra*?" The word was unfamiliar to me, although I remembered Beals telling me to avoid a man named Jiménez. "Is that the police?"

De Castro laughed mirthlessly. "No. There is also the National Police. They wear uniforms but are just as bad. Brigadier Ainciart is chief of the police. Jiménez is far more dangerous. His *Porristas* are a band of ruthless thugs and killers he established two years ago to terrorize anyone who opposes Machado's regime. *La Porra* has people everywhere. We must tread lightly, my friend, and not draw their attention. Jiménez can make your mission difficult." [9]

De Castro's words, more than Beals's vague warning, sent shivers along my spine. Being watched was one thing. Provoking *la Porra* was a chilling reality.

"When you say *difficult*," I pressed, the unease I felt clear in my voice, "what exactly do you think they would do to me?"

De Castro's gaze met mine, his words hanging ominously between us. "Their cruelty, it has no limits. Even an American is not beyond their reach if he becomes the target of Machado and his killers."

We drove in silence for a time, the weight of his words sinking in. I tried to enjoy the passing

---

[9] Little is known about Colonel Antonio Jiménez except that he formed *El Partido de la Porra* in 1931 as an unofficial branch of the Secret Police. He was murdered by members of Cuban military on 19 August, 1933 when President Machado fled the country. His body was burned and mutilated by the revolutionaries.

Havana scenery, but my mind held only one thought: *what have I gotten myself into?*

Seven

"GET DRESSED," de Castro's voice reverberated through the hotel door. "We are going to the Floridita!"

"Not tonight, José," I protested. I had just finished a simple dinner in the hotel restaurant and anticipated a long, hot bath.

"I want you to meet my journalist friends," he said after I opened the door. "They want to meet you. They are Americans, the men Señor Beals worked with when he was here last year. Come! We go!"

His eyes gleamed with an intensity that made resistance futile. De Castro's boundless energy compelled compliance. And so, against my better judgment, I yielded to his relentless persuasion. I found my coat and hat and descended to the ground floor in the creaking elevator.

As expected, de Castro's car waited outside. It was six blocks from my hotel to the Floridita, farther than one would care to walk. His car stopped in the small park I had noted before, and we joined the raucous crowd, their conversation and laughter mingling with the clinking of Daiquiri glasses and the rhythmic whoosh of the cocktail shakers.

As we waited for our frozen drinks, I noticed Hemingway at the far end of the bar, locked in conversation with a captivating blond, their heads nearly touching.

De Castro led me to a table occupied by two men. With coats hanging on the back of their chairs and collars and ties undone, both appeared to have already consumed multiple Daiquiris.

"Gentlemen," de Castro announced with a flourish as we took the vacant seats, "allow me to introduce Señor Walker Evans. He has come to Havana to immortalize in photographs what Señor Beals captured in words."

Indicating a slim man with thinning hair, de Castro continued. "Walker, this is Larry Haas, UP. If you need to know anyone in the Cuban government, he is your man."

Haas and I shook hands across the table. "Welcome to Havana, Evans. Your first time?"

Before I could respond, de Castro gestured toward the other man. "And this, of course, is the dean of American journalists in Cuba, J.D. Phillips, the *Times*. Nothing happens in Cuba that escapes Phil's notice."

Phillips was a serious-looking man with a round face and dark wavy hair brushed back from a bold forehead. He nodded in a friendly yet reserved way. One corner of his mouth turned up as if amused by something we were not privy to.

"My card," Phillips said, casually handing me an engraved card he pulled from his vest pocket. Appropriately enough, the fine cream-colored paper displayed his name and phone number in Times font. Keenly aware I didn't have one to return, I thanked him and tucked the card in my pocket.

J.D. Phillips [10] was a well-known name in the States. His *Times* dispatches rivaled Beals for colorful and inflammatory prose. Phillips was an influential critic of American Imperialistic involvement in Cuba, espousing a position aligned with Beals.

"So you're working for Beals?" Haas asked.

His tone was so friendly that I found it difficult to take exception to his assumption. "No," I replied firmly. "I am working for Lippincott. Ernestine Evans hired me. She believes Beals's book

---

10 James Doyle Phillips (1896—1937) was a freelance journalist for the *New York Times* in Cuba beginning in 1931. Following his death in an auto accident, his wife Ruby Hart Phillips (1898—1985) became the *Times* correspondent until the revolution in 1959.

will benefit from my perspective on what's happening here."

"The man is driven," Haas continued, referring to Beals. "Too driven, if you ask me. There is an edge of insanity to his work."

"He does write flamboyantly," Phillips interjected, tempering his friend's words with a touch of diplomacy. I sensed these two friends disagreed on many levels.

"Huh," Haas scoffed. "A good journalist balances his personal views and those of his employer. Something you have never learned, Phil."

Phillips' face darkened, accented by the dim lights overhead. "I write what I see," he said in a slow, drawn-out mid-western accent. "They publish it, or they don't. Beals was never going to accept your views of this country. He didn't kowtow to any bureaucrat."

"Fuck you," Haas said, tossing back the last of his drink. "I'll tell you what I think—Beals was damn lucky to get out of Cuba alive." Pushing up from the table, he stood weaving slightly and added, "I'll tell you who else needs to be careful—our new ambassador. If Welles doesn't watch his ass, he might find it handed to him by the ABC. Now, who needs another drink?"

He staggered to the bar without waiting for an answer, returning with four fresh glasses.

There didn't seem to be any hard feelings between the men, who launched into another heated discussion on American control of Cuban sugar prices.

I was preparing to tell de Castro I wanted to return to the hotel when a chair scraped beside me, and Ernest Hemingway dropped into it.

Looking relatively sober, he laid a heavy arm on my shoulder and asked, "Who are *you*?"

"This is Walker Evans, Papa," de Castro interjected. "I introduced you the other night."

Hemingway squinted at me, either trying to remember our meeting or determining if I was worth remembering. One eyebrow lifted. "The photographer of some renown!"

"Yes," I laughed, pleased to have made an impression. "In some circles. Not to the world at large, I'm afraid."

"Who cares," Hemingway said, squeezing the back of my neck. His hand was rough and powerful. "If you're good enough, the world will find you. What brings you to *La Habana*?"

I briefly explained my assignment.

"Carleton Beals?" Hemingway barked. "Now, there's a writer in need of an editor. I've read a couple of his books. Good stuff mostly, but too many fucking words."

I had to agree with Hemingway's assessment. Although Beals had refused to let me see his new book, I had read parts of *Mexican Maze* before, primarily because Rivera illustrated it.

Beals knew Mexico well, although he did go for the hyperbole. Nothing was grey or mundane. In that country, the colors are all sun-bright. The blacks are more than black; they are obsidian. The heroes are shiningly heroic, and the villains are the devil incarnate. I suspect his latest will be more of the same.

"I can't argue with that," I said. "It's funny we would meet in Havana."

"Why's that?" Hemingway asked, arching one eyebrow.

"I saw you a couple times in Paris. Once at Shakespeare and Company."

"You were in Paris?" Hemingway asked as if I couldn't possibly be old enough.

"Yes, in '26 and '27. I thought I wanted to be a writer. I believed there was no better place to become a writer than Paris."

Hemingway smiled wryly, a mischievous twinkle in his dark brown eyes. "And yet you became a photographer."

"Hmm. Yes, I did," I replied softly. Hemingway didn't hear what I said.

"You know," he continued, swirling the icy remains of his drink, "I love Paris. I married my wife there."

"I know. I saw you a day or so after your wedding."

Hemingway cocked his head. "Where would that have been?"

"You were having dinner at La Closerie des Lilas. Celebrating your wedding, I guess."

"More like celebrating the end of the old one." Hemingway grinned and squeezed my neck again. "You stalking me, kid?" he asked half in jest.

Not waiting for an answer, the writer swiveled in his chair toward Phillips. "Phil!" he shouted. "You shoulda seen the marlin I hooked today! A fucking monster, I tell you..."

And he was gone, telling Phillips about the afternoon on the *Anita*, the number of times the marlin breached before they could gaff it, and the glory of it all.

I sat back, partially listening to the story, while the guitar music played by an old man near the front door began to separate itself from the crowd's noise. The sad melody played on a classical six-string seeped into my head and heightened the melancholy I was already feeling.

I hadn't thought about Paris for a long time. Talking to Hemingway made me remember how lonely I had been.

And how much I loved it.

My mind drifted back to the fall of 1926, to a bustling cafe on the corner of Saint-Germain and rue Bonaparte, a requisite destination for every struggling artist in Paris—the iconic *Les Deux Magots.*

Paris, 1926

"Will there be anything else, sir?" the waiter asked pointedly.

The man had been hovering near my table since I placed my empty tea cup back on its saucer. Waiters at Les Deux Magots were skilled at tactfully ushering away lingering patrons.

"Un autre thé, s'il te plaît," I said with what I knew to be a perfect accent. The waiter smirked and retreated to the service stand. Despite my excellent French, he always insisted on speaking to me in English.

I resumed my morning ritual of observing the famous and soon-to-be-famous who frequented the café. A fine drizzle wet the streets, bringing down the last of the orange Sycamore leaves and compelling the Magots' patrons to seek shelter under the protective canopy.

Two tables away, F. Scott Fitzgerald, another regular, engaged in a heated conversation with Dorothy Parker. His attire was as impeccable as ever, his hair slicked and parted in the middle with razor-sharp accuracy.

Dorothy was older than he, mid-thirties, with strikingly large dark eyes. She scrutinized Fitzgerald with an intensity that would make any man jealous.

Suddenly, she frowned and rose, her chair falling over. "You know I hate it when you're like this, Scott. You've got to stop!" Then, she threw her napkin on the table and marched into the rain, her umbrella snapping open defiantly.

"Dottie, stay," he pleaded, but she was already gone.

Ignoring the whispers, Fitzgerald straightened his silverware as the waiter swiftly picked up the chair and removed Dorothy's untouched meal.

Such was the daily drama that drew us all to this hallowed ground—a theater of literary giants, some more intoxicated than others, and I had a front-row seat. I absorbed it all, basking in their radiance and dreaming I would one day join their ranks.

I'd come to Paris to find my creative spirit and become a great writer. However, the city's allure proved a constant distraction. Museums, galleries, the opera—I spent my father's fifteen-dollar-a-week stipend freely while attending the occasional class at the Sorbonne.

Then, I discovered that small corner of Paris and made it my late-morning haunt. One day, I sat next to T.S. Eliot and a young woman as they discussed the mental decline of Eliot's wife, Vivienne. Later, I discovered that his companion was his niece, Theodora, who strongly defended her aunt against Eliot's criticism.

It was not far-fetched to assume the young woman, or Dorothy Parker for that matter, was having an affair with any of these men. It was Paris, after all. It was expected. Sex lingered in the air. The city exuded an inescapable sensuality that both thrilled and terrified me. I felt it everywhere, but capturing it in my writing remained elusive.

Deux Magots was not the only place where I whiled away my time. A short walk from Madam Thuilier's pension to 12 rue de l'Odéon was the renowned Shakespeare and Company bookstore.

I recall the day I summoned the courage to venture inside. My heart pounded as I navigated the overcrowded shelves deeper into the store. The intoxicating scent of old books mingled with the faint aroma of tobacco, almost overwhelming me. It was simultaneously thrilling and disheartening. So many books…

On any given day, you could encounter a titan of literature, those Gertrude Stein called the Lost Generation— Hemingway, Dos Passos, T.S. Eliot,

Fitzgerald, and more—engaged in academic discussions or everyday gossip. Being in their presence and breathing the same air was both exhilarating and frightening.

Sylvia Beach [11] opened the bookstore in 1919. Three years later, she secured her place in literary history by publishing *Ulysses*. Despite being a masterpiece of modernism, the novel was banned in many countries, including the United States, on ludicrous obscenity charges. Was I a fool to believe I could ever write like that?

Dressed in her customary brown velvet smoking jacket and slacks, a cigarette dangling from her lips, Sylvia effortlessly worked the floor as if hosting a perpetual cocktail party. She moved swiftly, her light brown eyes constantly darting from one visitor to another. Here, an encouraging word to a struggling writer; there, a recommendation to a curious tourist.

She was one of the nicest people I ever met.

I spent so much time lingering in the bookstore that Sylvia took me under her maternal wing, allowing me to eavesdrop on the simplistic, pedantic, surreal, or enlightened conversations in

---

11 Nancy Woodbridge 'Sylvia' Beach (1887—1962), was an American-born bookseller and publisher who lived most of her life in Paris, where she was a leading expatriate figure between the World Wars. Shakespear and Company is a favorite tourist destination to this day, but it is not in the original location.

which her famous patrons engaged. Ultimately, I spent more time listening to intellectual conversations and reading great literature than writing my own.

I saw Ernest Hemingway twice in Paris. On the first occasion, I had no idea who he was. He and Dorothy Parker, the epitome of wit and sophistication, sat in the back corner of Shakespeare, discussing the man with whom she was having an affair in graphically uncomplimentary terms. It was only later, when the whole world knew Hemingway's name, I realized it was him.

From my vantage point, I learned that Hemingway was unimpressed with F. Scott Fitzgerald's introspective style. He thought little of Fitzgerald's latest novel, *The Great Gatsby*, which I considered a masterpiece. Furthermore, he added in a hushed voice that I strained to overhear, the man won't be able to satisfy you in bed. How much of this personal critique stemmed from jealousy has sparked endless debates. How could Hemingway possibly know Fitzgerald's prowess in bed? [12]

Hemingway's masterpiece, *The Sun Also Rises*, was published later that year, establishing the two men as lifelong literary rivals caught between an on-again, off-again friendship.

---

12 See *A Movable Feast* for the answer to that question.

The second time I saw Hemingway was in May 1927, days before my return to New York. Treating myself to an extravagant dinner of panfried steak in creamy whiskey sauce at La Closerie des Lilas, I recognized Ernest Hemingway and his new bride, Pauline. Hemingway was now the talk of Paris, though not all in a good way. While his novel had taken the literary world by storm, there were those who felt it described his friends and acquaintances far too accurately. He gathered fans in equal measure to the friends he lost.

As they ate a late supper, more than one admirer asked to have their copy of his novel autographed. I contemplated approaching the author until my innate shyness overcame me, and the moment passed.

My inability to approach well-known people has haunted me my entire life. However, on one occasion, this anxiety saved me from humiliating myself before my idol.

The Master, James Joyce, could always be found at a small writing table at the back of the bookstore. No ordinary person dared to approach him uninvited. He was the Zeus of the Parisian *literati*, and the bookstore was his Olympus.

One afternoon, Sylvia offered to introduce me. Panic-stricken, I declined, and thank God I did.

Sometime later, I witnessed another unfortunate soul sit before the throne. Trembling with awe, the young man described his writing, his dreams, and his love of *Ulysses*.

Joyce sat impassively, saying nothing, his delicate hands folded on a book. When the young man ran out of words and stuttered to a stop, Joyce said, "Hmm," and returned to his reading.

The young man fled in terror. I watched him bolt into the street, thinking: that could have been me.

The story I told Ambassador Welles about my interaction with Joyce was a lie. I never spoke to Joyce and was forever thankful for it. The brittle faith in my own artistry would not have survived.

As the months passed, I spent less time in class and more time wandering the streets, idling at Deux Magots or de Flore, or reading at Shakespeare and Company. The writing I managed to produce consisted primarily of essays and translations of the French masters.

Studying Flaubert, I learned that beauty resides in the details that often escape the average eye. Baudelaire showed me that the street itself was the museum of humanity—a sharp corner of a building, the posters plastered against the wall, every girder and angle of the Eiffel Tower conveyed a story that needed no words. I was never without my trusty camera. It spoke for me where words failed.

I departed Paris with a newfound perspective and a revitalized sense of purpose. Although I yearned to be a great writer, deep down, I knew it was not my destiny. The time spent in the presence of greatness had made that abundantly clear. The camera had become my passion; through its lens, I would discover my true calling.

"Where ya been, kid," Hemingway shook me by the arm, jolting me back to the present. "So, tell me about your photos. They any good?"

Still dreaming of France, his abrupt return to our previous conversation caught me off guard. I muttered, "I'm trying."

"Has anybody seen them? You know, there's nothing wrong with creating art for yourself. Matter of fact, you should *only* do it for yourself. But even artists want a pat on the back now and then."

"Well," I said, "I had a show at the Becker Gallery in New York."

"Anybody come?"

I nodded. "It was well attended. I shared space with Margaret Bourke-White."

"Huh," Hemingway shrugged. "Never heard of her."

"And," I continued, "I illustrated a book of poems that used the Brooklyn Bridge as a metaphor for America as a whole."

"Christ almighty. Was it any good?"

"I couldn't say. Critics were mixed in their reviews. It was extremely long, though. It was by my friend Hart Crane."

"Hah!" Hemingway exploded, slapping the table. "I *have* seen your photos! Grant Mason gave me that book. God knows why. I don't know if his writing was good. I didn't care for it. Poetry or prose, if it doesn't move me, I can't read it. What's he working on now?"

"Nothing," I said, dropping my eyes, the pain sudden and intense. "Hart killed himself last year. He jumped off a ship coming back from Mexico."

Hemingway rubbed the back of my neck again. "Christ. Sorry, kid. But, I'll tell you, I think probably the best way would be to go off an ocean liner at night. The ocean beneath you, the stars above."

We sat silently, each contemplating death. Then he said, "I like you, kid. How 'bout you come round my hotel tomorrow? Say 'bout five? We'll have a drink. Hell, we'll have two!"

With that, he turned back to the table and shouted, "That's bullshit!" to no one in particular.

Eight

THE HOTEL AMBOS MUNDOS was two blocks from my hotel. As I walked along Obispo, I tried to calm the butterflies in my stomach. It was one thing to drink in a bar with the famous Ernest Hemingway and quite another to be invited to join him in his hotel room.

His hotel, painted a dull coral color, was an eclectic architecture unique to Havana. I couldn't identify a specific style. Small balconies flanked the flat front corner of the building, while the rooms on each side had balustrade railings. The large, high-ceilinged lobby was cool and dark, allowing the residents to observe the street unnoticed and enjoy a cigar from wing-back chairs.

I took the cage elevator to the fifth floor and knocked on the door of room 501. [13]

"It's open!" came the shout from within.

---

[13] Years later, the Hotel Ambos Mundos renumbered their rooms and made Hemingway's famous abode Room 511, which it is today.

Ernest Hemingway sat at a small table in front of *portes-fenêtres* that opened to a fine view north, over the massive walls of the *Palacio de los Capitanes Generales*, to Morro Castle in the distance, and the sea beyond. Light curtains ruffled in the breeze. The classical balustrade I had noted from the street prevented anyone from plummeting to the pavement.

The writer wore a stained undershirt and shorts and was in his bare feet. Papers were scattered on the table beside a battered Corona typewriter while others drifted around the ornately tiled floor.

Other than the writing table, the only furniture in the room was a single bed in a niche near the second set of French doors and a scarred yellow dresser against the far wall. The austere room was not what I expected. For a man of such stature, in every sense of the word, I had envisioned far more luxurious accommodations.

"Good," Hemingway said, twisting in his chair to face me. "You found me."

"Yes," I replied, feeling slightly overwhelmed to be alone in his presence. "Thank you for inviting me, Mr. Hemingway."

"Call me Papa! Pour yourself a drink." He gestured toward the dresser. "I started without you."

I found an empty glass and a half-empty bottle of Old Forester on the piece he indicated. Even though bourbon wasn't my favorite drink, I poured myself two fingers to fortify my courage. Hemingway held out his glass, and I filled it halfway.

Clearing my throat, I said, "This is a pleasant room. Do you always stay here?" I found it difficult to call him *Papa*, so I avoided proper nouns altogether.

Looking around the room, Hemingway said, "Since last year when I came over from Key West with Joe. I like the view, and I like the solitude. I have my routine. Every morning, I pull on an old pair of khaki pants and a shirt, take the pair of moccasins that are dry...walk to the elevator, ride down, get a paper at the desk, walk across the corner to the café to have breakfast."

"Sounds very comfortable," I said, taking a tentative sip of bourbon. It burned my throat, but I liked the flavor.

"You may find it hard to believe, kid," he said, "but I'm a solitary man at heart."

Having observed him interact with tourists and regulars at the Floridita, I did find it hard to believe. Hemingway's reputation as a hard-drinking, full-throttle man's man was known the world over. I wondered how much of that persona was an act and how much was real. Seeing him now, I believed it to be the former.

And there was his way of calling me 'kid.' Hemingway was three years my senior, yet he seemed much older. Or, maybe I felt that much younger.

Still standing awkwardly, I pointed to the papers on his writing desk and ventured, "Are you working on a new novel?"

He looked at his desk as if noticing the sheets for the first time. "This? No," he growled. "I'm fighting with that bastard Eastman. Can you believe it? He reviews *Death in the Afternoon* and calls me a *fairy*. In print! I'm going to bury the son of a bitch."

My lack of understanding must have shown on my face. "Max Eastman?" Hemingway continued. "Writes for *The New Republic*. He had the gall to say the book exposes my sexual insecurities. He called my book 'Bull in the Afternoon.' Insecurities! I'll show him how insecure I am next time we're in the same room together…"

Hemingway stopped abruptly and slammed back the remainder of his bourbon. "Fuck him. Gimme another, kid," he said, holding out his glass. I emptied the last of the bottle. His anger at Eastman dissipated as quickly as it had appeared.

The popping sound of several consecutive pistol shots echoed through the open window.

Hemingway ignored it—just another evening in Havana.

He waved at the bed. "Have a seat. Sorry, there's no other chairs."

I perched on the edge of the bed. It felt unyielding, and the springs squeaked when I moved. "Get any good pictures today?" he continued after a moment of silence.

I was delighted to discuss my work and had almost finished describing how I spent the day when a scraping outside the window startled me. As a question formed on my lips, the most amazing sight one could imagine unfolded before my eyes.

A beautiful young woman dressed in a white blouse and tan skirt stood on the ledge encircling the fifth floor.

"Good Lord!" I gasped, rising from the bed.

Hemingway sprang to his feet and helped the woman climb over the railing and enter the room.

"Hello, daughter," he greeted her as if they had encountered each other on the street.

The woman brushed back a strand of loose blond hair and kissed Hemingway on the cheek. I'm certain I stood there with my mouth hanging open.

"Hello, Papa," she responded in an equally casual manner. "Who's this, then?" she asked, extending her hand. I shook it in a daze.

"Jane, meet Walker Evans, a photographer of some renown. Evans, this cool drink is Jane Mason." [14]

"How do you do, Mr. Evans?" she purred, her voice richly modulated. I was unable to form a coherent response and merely nodded in return.

Jane Mason may have been the most beautiful creature I ever met. She was tall and athletically trim with strawberry blond hair pulled back in a bun and wide-set grey-blue eyes. Her face was perfectly oval, so perfect that one might question her intelligence. That would be a mistake. I soon discovered that this elegant twenty-three-year-old was wise beyond her years.

And incredibly fragile.

I peeked over the railing to see how she had reached the room. The brick ledge was no more than twenty inches wide. There were no handholds. A misstep would result in a straight drop to the pavement seventy feet below. Just looking at it made my head spin.

"Jane often takes the room next to this one," Hemingway said as if that explained her action.

---

14 Jane Kendall Mason (1909–1981) was a debutante, socialite, and outdoorswoman. At a young age, she showed promise in drawing and sculpture and competed as an equestrian. At eighteen, she married Geroge Grant Mason, a wealthy Yale graduate, who served as head of Pan American Airways' Caribbean operations in Cuba.

"She comes over to distract me. We believe no one should see her coming or going."

"And it's terribly fun!" Jane added brightly.

I found it impossible to believe that the sight of a blond woman traversing a ledge five stories above the ground would attract less attention than being spotted in the hallway. I suspected it was more of a game they played than any need for secrecy.

Struggling not to stare, I couldn't shake the feeling I had seen this woman before. Her face, with those captivating blue eyes, was not easily forgotten.

Then it hit me.

Standing right before me was the face of Pond's Beauty Cream. Her advertisement promoting the allure of a healthy tan had been a major marketing success in New York. This socialite beauty almost singlehandedly transformed the perception of women being outdoors, basking in the sun, from something frowned upon to something acceptable and desirable.

"So, where's Grant tonight?" Hemingway asked Jane. Then, for my benefit, he added, "Jane's husband is an executive at Pan American. He runs the Caribbean office."

"Oh," Jane said as if bored with whatever her husband was doing, "I left him at Jaimanitas with his dreary airline executives."

"Shouldn't you be there?"

"Probably," she said, plopping onto the foot of the bed. I may have blushed at her boldness and tried not to picture her on that bed in other circumstances. "He'll get over it. Besides, we're hosting a party tomorrow night for all of them, their wives, or mistresses—whichever they decide to bring. You'll come, won't you? It will be unbearable if you're not there. And you too, Mr. Evans!"

"Walker, please," I said.

She flashed a brilliant smile at me. "Walker, it is! I see the bottle is empty, Papa. Are we going out or not?"

"Out, of course," Hemingway said, pulling on a dark cotton shirt and shoes. He held out a hand to Jane, and she rose from the bed as if accepting an invitation to dance.

She hooked one arm in his and the other in mine. "Such an escort! No woman could ask for more!"

The Floridita was packed and bustling as usual. A four-man band played loud American jazz, and the volume of conversations strived to match it.

Within a minute of our arrival, a bartender appeared with three drinks, knowing we would have Daiquiris.

An hour later, Hemingway and Jane were on their third. My first drink was still in my hand. Another melted on the table before me.

"So," Jane asked as we sipped our drinks, "who's Walker Evans?"

I could have been the only other person in the room at that moment. I took a deep breath and described my project and my goal of capturing the essence of Cuba in my own unique way. She listened intently, chin propped on her hand, elbow on the table. Smoke from her cigarette drifted between us.

She was more intoxicating than the Daiquiris.

"That's what you're doing," Jane said when I fell silent. "I asked *who* is Walker Evans. You grew up in the mid-west, am I right?"

"And here I thought my accent was refined New Yorker," I joked, blushing at her intuition. "Yes, I was born in St. Louis and grew up in Chicago and Toledo, Ohio. I moved to New York after my parents split."

"And your parents, are they still living?"

A jolt went through me, and I took a drink, suddenly realizing I didn't want to discuss my family or my early life. I didn't want to talk about my father's recent death or the fact that he had left my mother to move in with the woman next door when I was fourteen. Jane didn't need to know that his influence on my life was the equivalent of being thrown into the pool's deep end — learn to swim or drown. Sure, he occasionally provided money, allowing me to live in Paris or buy a camera, but he was never part of my life after he left. Nor did he appreciate my artistic calling, telling me more than once that I was wasting my life and should get a paying job.

Still —

I wish he had lived long enough to see my first exhibition.

"My mother's alive," I said flatly. "Neither of my parents appreciated my art. I've been on my own for a long time."

"Jane is an artist, too," Hemingway interjected from the sideline.

Jane straightened, sitting back in her chair.

"Really? What do you do?" I asked, sensing the tension between them.

She gave Hemingway a hard look before responding. "I have a second-story studio at our house in Jaimanitas. It is cool and always has a wonderful breeze. It's my sanctuary."

"Jane is learning to be a sculptor," Hemingway explained. "There isn't anything this girl can't do once she sets her mind to it."

"Nothing?" I asked.

"She shoots, rides horses, fishes better than most men, and doesn't care who knows it."

He was obviously proud of Jane's accomplishments and fiercely protective of her. It would go badly for any man who came between them. I wondered if that included her husband.

A little later, Jane announced she wanted to dance. "Papa doesn't like to dance here," she said, fixing her eyes on me. "He says a bar is for drinking. Does Walker Evans dance?"

I did dance, but I had no intention of doing so tonight, especially with Hemingway sitting right there.

Jane frowned at our lassitude and approached a table of young Cuban men. They were not intimidated by her beauty or her famous companion. Hemingway and I observed for a few minutes, then he turned his back on her. The men in the bar scrutinized her every move.

I noted the scowl on Hemingway's face. "You okay with her dancing like that?"

"She's not my wife," he said flatly.

"And where is your wife?" I asked, immediately regretting the question.

Hemingway gave me a hard look, then said, "*My* wife is with *her* husband. Pauline sometimes stays with the Masons when she's here. Doesn't like the Mundos."

Deciding it was best to change the subject, I asked Hemingway if he had ever heard of Diego Rivera.

"Of course. He's painting a mural in New York. Read about it in the *Havana Post*."

"A few days before I left New York, they ordered the mural destroyed."

Hemingway's eyes narrowed, his passion for art evident in his response. "Who did?" he snapped.

"Rockefeller, I suppose," I answered. "Diego put Lenin's face in the mural to protest against some critics who said the mural was anti-capitalist."

Hemingway's face showed a flash of anger. "That's a goddamn shame. If you hire an artist, you need to stay the hell out of his way."

"People were upset," I added.

"You mean *Rockefeller* was upset," Hemingway corrected me. "It's the same thing. People don't get to say. Art isn't for the people."

In time to hear the last comment, Jane fell back into her chair, smiling broadly. A sheen of perspiration made her face glow. "What are you saying, Papa? An artist doesn't have to answer to anyone? Art for art's sake?"

Hemingway's gaze intensified as he elaborated. "No. Art. Period. Nothing matters beyond the art. It doesn't matter who makes it. A fucking monkey can paint a picture, but if it's good, it's good. If someone doesn't like it, that's their problem."

Jane looked at me, a playful smile on her lips. "Do you agree, Walker? Do you have the final say in your art? Are you photographing what you want or what your employer wants?"

That was a question I had been wrestling with. Was I here to provide photographic evidence for Beals's book or to capture what I felt was the real Cuba? In reality, I wasn't accomplishing either. I was doing what de Castro wanted.

"In the end," I said tentatively, "I hope to do both. While I may have a free hand, I'm being paid by my employer to produce something they can use."

Jane squinted at me for a moment. "Which will it be, Walker?"

I paused, thinking of a good answer, but none came. "I'll know when I see it," I said.

Jane considered my response before saying, "You're smarter than you look, aren't you? I like you."

At that moment, an older Cubano gentleman came to the table, bowed to Hemingway, and extended his hand to Jane. She gave Hemingway a what-can-I-do smile and rose from her chair.

As the night wore on, all eyes in the packed bar were on Jane. She danced with a mesmerizing energy, her uninhibited nature on full display. She outshined all the other women.

"That's quite a girl," I ventured, the alcohol loosening my tongue more than it should.

"She's the biggest ball-buster I've ever met," Hemingway growled.

"I can believe that."

His voice barely audible over the music, Hemingway added, "She's also the most uninhibited woman I've ever known. No man could resist that."

The night air was hazy as we stumbled out of the bar, our steps unsteady from the countless drinks. It was too far to walk in our condition, so we hailed a taxi. I stayed with them until we reached the Ambos Mundos. I intended to walk to my hotel from there—to try and walk off the rum.

Hemingway paid the fare and waited for Jane, leaning against the wall for support. Jane, her fiery spirit still burning, gave me a mischievous smile. "Want to join us?" she asked softly.

"For a drink?" I asked cautiously, trying to make sense of her invitation.

"It's a good place to start," she whispered, her eyes smoldering, her lips slightly parted.

My heart raced, torn between opposing emotions. Before I could form an answer, Hemingway abruptly straightened and lurched toward us. "Get lost, Evans!" he growled in a burst of drunken anger.

Jane softly kissed my cheek, her lips lingering for just a moment. "Goodnight, Mr. Evans," she murmured.

She took Hemingway's arm, and they disappeared into the hotel.

That was the last time I ever saw Jane Mason.

Two days later, she tried to kill herself.

Nine

DE CASTRO MENTIONED Jane's "accident" as we drove through the city. Unaware of my evening spent with her and Hemingway, he said the circumstances of her fall from her studio balcony were unclear.

I was shocked. "Will she be okay?" I asked, my voice reflecting my concern.

De Castro gave me a questioning look and shrugged. "Don't know. I heard she broke her back and must go to New York for treatment."

"What happened?" I asked.

"They say she may have been—what do you say, sneaking?—sneaking out of her house to meet Señor Hemingway at his hotel and fell."

I pictured her negotiating a narrow ledge five stories in the air to reach her lover's hotel room. It was impossible to imagine this graceful and athletic woman falling off anything.

"There are whispers," de Castro continued, "by others who claim she threw herself from the balcony in a fit of rage, a desperate attempt to end her own life."

"It's hard to believe," I said. Then, upon reflection, I realized that perhaps it wasn't so unbelievable after all. There was a deep sadness in Jane Mason. But I would not have expected her to try and kill herself. In the short time I knew her, she gave the impression of someone living precariously on the edge and enjoying the danger. I could not stop picturing her haunting smile and the intensity in her eyes as she kissed me goodnight.

De Castro noticed my silence. "You know this woman," he stated cautiously.

"Yes. She's extraordinary," I said and left it at that.

I hadn't been back to the Floridita since my evening with Jane and Hemingway. My days were busy and exhausting. De Castro's boundless energy kept me occupied as he chatted away, always suggesting another location that would "make a wonderful photograph!"

During one of our stops, I commented on the sedan parked half a block away. I was certain I had seen it earlier and wondered if it was following us.

"Ignore it," de Castro said dismissively. "It is to be expected."

When I looked later, the sedan was gone.

At de Castro's insistence, I photographed scenes of everyday life in Cuba—people queuing for bread, lottery booths displaying the previous day's winning numbers, a cart laden with colorful fresh fruit, and a movie theater showing the adaptation of *A Farewell to Arms.*

When I next saw Hemingway, I asked him his opinion of Hollywood's take on his masterpiece. He said it was an abomination, although he liked the performance of the young actor Gary Cooper.[15]

While my photographs were good and technically proficient, I felt I was failing to capture what I really needed. Where were the images that would support Beals's claims of corruption and oppression inflicted by Machado's regime? Where was the evidence of murder and thuggery that supposedly plagued the country?

I had witnessed nothing like that. The photos I took could have been taken by any tourist on any given day. Apart from the brief scuffle at the

---

15 Frank James 'Gary' Cooper (1901—1961) was a two-time Oscar winner known for his laconic acting style. He and Hemingway met in 1940 and became great friends. Cooper died seven weeks before Hemingway.

wreath-laying ceremony, I had seen little to convince me that Cuba suffered at Machado's hands.

That illusion of innocence would soon be shattered.

The first signs of trouble went unnoticed. It wasn't until a gunshot pierced the air, shattering the calm, that I realized how exposed we were.

De Castro and I were in the process of setting up my camera on the sidewalk across from the Movietone theater. Colorful billboards adorned the archways. One promoted the Warner Baxter thriller *Six Hours to Live*. The adjacent arch showcased Edward G. Robinson's biopic *Silver Dollar*. Its Spanish title was *El Rey de la Plata*, a more accurate description of Colorado silver tycoon Horace Tabor.

As I focused the lens, my head hidden beneath the cloth, the first shouts erupted. Three young men, cigarettes dangling casually from their lips, leaned against a nearby building. Two agitated policemen barked orders, yet the men remained defiant, their insolence visible from a distance. And then, with a flick of his cigarette butt, one of the men deliberately provoked the officers.

In an instant, the entire situation changed. The young man's insult drove the enraged policeman to raise his baton, preparing to strike. Before he could act, the man stepped forward and delivered a powerful blow to the policeman's chin. The officer crumpled to the ground as if he had been shot. Without hesitation, the second policeman drew his pistol and fired point-blank at the assailant.

Panic engulfed the scene as people scattered in all directions. Those waiting to enter the theater surged through its doors, seeking a safe haven. The two remaining men raced around the nearest corner, abandoning their wounded companion, who lay bleeding in the street.

I stood, open-mouthed, while de Castro grabbed my camera and ran toward an open-air restaurant.

"Where is your driver?" I panted as we entered the bodega. "Let's get out of here!"

"No time," de Castro said, also breathing hard. "We need to be off the street." With that, he sat at an unoccupied table hidden behind the brick arch support. A handful of patrons warily eyed the scene unfolding in the street.

Moments later, a siren blared, and a police car screeched to a stop. By then, the fallen policeman had regained his feet. The man who had been shot remained motionless where he had fallen. A crimson stain spread on the cobblestones and ran into the gutter.

Next to our table, a man well into his seventies continued to devour a plate of black beans and yellow rice, unfazed by what had happened. His dark, creased face and ragged, filthy clothes spoke of hardship and poverty. A stubble of white beard covered his chin. Noting my attention, the wooden spoon paused partway to his mouth, and he spoke in flawless English.

"This is no place for a *norteamericano*," he said, his words filled with urgency. "You should leave."

I couldn't agree more. Quickly checking on the action in the street, I asked, "Why would they care about me? I am just a tourist taking pictures of Havana."

"*Why?*" The old man seemed to question my intelligence with that one word. "You are here. That is the only reason they need." Accepting that we were not leaving until the incident on the corner was resolved, he smiled, displaying strong, white teeth. "So tell me, *norteamericano*, why *are* you here?"

I briefly explained what I was trying to capture with my photographs and the soon-to-be-published book exposing the current regime. When I mentioned Beals's name, the old man looked surprised.

"I met the man you speak of, Señor Beals," he said matter-of-factly.

"You met Carleton Beals?" I asked, the skepticism evident in my voice. "How did that happen, if I may ask?"

"He came to the docks where I work. To interview us," he replied. "He wanted to know what I thought of our *Presidente*. He told me of his book and how it would change the world's view of Cuba—and the United States."

I was completely taken aback by this statement. This elderly gentleman, for that is what he truly was, appeared to have emerged from a coal mine, yet he possessed a sophistication that belied his appearance.

"What did you tell him?" I asked, finding it difficult to accept his story.

"We discussed Machado, of course," he said, his intelligent eyes filled with passion. "I also told him that Machado was merely a fraction of Cuba's troubles."

"Please," I said, turning my attention from the street where the police were loading a lifeless body into the back of a white ambulance, "tell me what you said."

"I explained," the old man continued, "that the ultimate crime is that after four hundred years, Cuba is still without true sovereignty and that the United States strengthens Machado's tyranny while doing nothing to restrain his violent excesses."

I sat in stunned silence, absorbing his words. "Who *are* you?" I finally managed to ask.

"I am nobody," he sighed, his voice heavy with a lifetime of sadness. "Once, I taught English and mathematics at a secondary school. Then, when I spoke out against Machado, I was arrested. I lost my job. Afterwards, no school would hire me. Today, I work at the docks loading coal." The old man paused and lifted his empty glass to me. "A glass of rum, perhaps? My throat is dry."

I raised my hand to the waiter, who had not yet approached our table. "*Tres rones por favor*," I said, and he brought clean glasses and a bottle of Bacardi. The waiter nervously eyed the street, poured our drinks, and retreated behind the counter. The three of us toasted silently and downed the rum in one swallow. The warmth of the alcohol helped calm my rattled nerves.

The old man coughed and continued his lecture. "After the war with Spain came America ... To *free* us, you said ... All you did was steal victory from our grasp ... Free Cuba? ... Ha! ... We are bound by your dollars, by your bankers, by your greedy politicians who pose as statesmen ... Freedom? ... Our government, our *Presidente*, is nothing more than a puppet ... For all the blood and sacrifice of our people, and yes, your people too, we merely exchanged one master for another

... We are exiles in our own land ... That is the crime of Cuba, my friend."

During this unusual exchange, de Castro had been watching the street for signs of more trouble. "We go!" he said, his voice filled with alarm. He went to the counter and handed the waiter some coins.

Before we could leave, two men, clad in well-tailored dark suits and fedoras pulled low over their brows, entered the cantina. The old man stiffened, averting his eyes and concentrating on his meal.

One man stationed himself by the archway while the other approached our table with a pompous air of authority. Addressing me, he unleashed a rapid stream of Spanish, none of which I understood.

"I'm sorry," I stammered, feeling my palms grow damp. "I don't speak Spanish."

The man faced de Castro, repeating his words in a more threatening tone. De Castro responded, his voice measured and tinged with disdain. I suspected their conversation pertained to me.

Without warning, the man seized de Castro by the arm, forcefully spinning him around and pressing his body against the counter. His hands swept over de Castro, apparently searching for a weapon. Then, the man spun the journalist to face him, their eyes locked in a battle of defiance and resentment.

De Castro spoke softly, his words dripping with contempt. In response, the man, whom I now suspected to be a member of the feared *Porra*, delivered a stinging slap to de Castro's cheek. His face flushed with a mixture of anger and resentment. A snarl formed at the edges of his lips, but he maintained his composure.

Without another word, the two thugs strode back to the corner where the shooting had occurred.

"What was that all about," I asked when we were a block away and close to our car.

De Castro marched ahead without answering, seething with anger and, I suspected, a sense of humiliation.

"José?" I called out.

He stopped abruptly, his body tense, and faced me. "You see how it is? *La Porristas,* they use any excuse to harass citizens, especially journalists. They know me. They know I had nothing to do with that shooting, yet they use any opportunity to remind me of my position."

"Why did he strike you," I asked as we continued walking.

"I called him Machado's *perra*, his bitch."

"What?" I yelped. "You're lucky he didn't shoot you."

De Castro laughed without humor. "There is still time. Perhaps you should not walk too close to me!"

Driving to the hotel, I glanced out the rear window. The black sedan was back.

Ten

THE RAIN-SOAKED STREETS glistened under the glow of the streetlights as I walked up Calle Obispo to the Floridita. I needed a drink, and the Floridita was the place to have it.

De Castro had left me at the hotel and begged off, saying there was something he couldn't postpone. I suspected he was still stinging from the insulting slap on the face and didn't want to see any of his compadres.

Just ahead of another downpour, I ducked inside and found Hemingway sitting at the end of the bar, his rugged figure slouched over, engaged in conversation with Constante, the bar's owner.

When he saw me, he nodded without enthusiasm and beckoned me over. I took the stool next to him, tucked into the corner. Without asking, a Daiquiri materialized.

"I heard about Jane," I offered cautiously. "I'm so sorry. I hope she will be alright."

Hemingway's response was a fleeting smile, failing to hide his pain. His face was drawn, his eyes dull. "Grant says she needs surgery," he muttered, swallowing half his Daiquiri. "He's sending her back to New York. What a fucked up mess."

"You'll miss her," I said, stating the obvious.

"More than you know, kid. More than you know."

I didn't know what else to say, so we sat in silence, the raucous noise of the Floridita fading into the background.

Hemingway eventually turned to me, a fresh drink in his hand.

"Jane's not the only bad news. Did you hear this? Last week in Munich, thirty thousand Nazis held a book-burning party. Can you imagine? Thousands of books burned because Nazi officials said they weren't *German* enough. I heard they even burned my books! I tell you, kid, we'll be fighting those bastards again before much longer." He swallowed his drink in one gulp and raised the empty glass to Constante. "Burning books! Christ, what's next?"

He shook his head in disgust. Then, "I had a hell of a great day fishing," he said with forced enthusiasm.

I recognized his attempt to discuss any subject other than Jane and Nazis and feigned interest. "You fish for marlin, don't you? Catching a fish that big must be quite a thrill."

Hemingway straightened his shoulders. "You know, kid," he began, warming to the story. "There's nothing better than landing one of those monsters. It's always a battle, and you don't always win. That's an important lesson in life." He paused a moment, lost in thought. Then he said, "You fight the fish, and the fish fights you. Sometimes, the fish gets away. You can't feel sorry for yourself when the fish wins."

"You have your own boat?" I asked.

Hemingway smiled wistfully. "No, I've been coming over from Key West with Joe Russell. Joe's got a damned nice fishing boat—thirty-four-foot Redwing cabin cruiser called the *Anita*."

"All the way from Key West?" I asked, trying to imagine being in the open ocean in such a small boat. The thought made me shudder. "How long does it take you?"

"If the weather's on our side, we can make it in ten hours. Joe used to smuggle rum out of Cuba, so he knows these currents and winds like a man knows every curve of his lover's body."

I listened as he recounted his fishing expeditions, captivated by his animated storytelling. His eyes brightened as the pain of Jane's accident was momentarily forgotten.

I was pleased to have helped lift his spirits.

"I've got a new fishing guide this trip," Hemingway continued. "Fella named Carlos

Gutierrez. He's teaching me to set bait for different depths, something I never knew. He knows these waters as well as Joe knows the Gulf Stream." Hemingway took another drink, his eyes bright with mischief, and said, "Say, why don't you come out with us tomorrow? Feel the thrill of the hunt."

Caught off guard, I hesitated, torn between the desire to spend more time with Hemingway, memories of my South Pacific adventure, and my dislike of the ocean. "Thank you," I said, "I've had enough time on boats. Just the thought of it makes me queasy. I'm dreading my return trip to New York."

Hemingway laughed heartily, the sound echoing around the bar. I don't think my reluctance diminished me in his eyes at all.

"Remember what I told you—we're tied up at the old San Francisco Wharf in case you change your mind. Ask for Joe or Carlos. They're always on the boat, night or day. Unless they're off drinking."

I said, "I'll consider it."

Hemingway smiled benevolently. "That's okay, kid. The sea's not for everyone. But you're missing out. Good fishing, lots of drinking, and fine companions. That Carlos, I'll tell ya, he tells amazing stories. Today, he told me about this old fisherman who went out in a skiff and hooked the biggest marlin he had ever snagged, one so big it pulled him out to sea. Two days later, fishermen found the old man sixty miles east of here. Sixty miles! The old man had stayed with the fish day and night. When he finally harpooned it and lashed it alongside, the sharks attacked the fish, and the old man fought them off, clubbing and stabbing at them. Carlos said the old man was crying when the fishermen picked him up, half-crazy from his loss. The sharks were still circling the boat."

I am sure I listened wide-eyed, fully appreciating Hemingway's ability to tell a simple tale in a way you could picture it, smell it, taste it. The man was a master storyteller.

"That's an incredible story," I said. "Will you write it?"

"Maybe," he waved a calloused hand dismissively as if shooing a mosquito, "Who can say? I've written stories about fishing, and it was good stuff, mostly. But you have to experience fishing firsthand. You see, it's not just the act of reeling them in. It's the struggle, the connection you forge with the fish. Same with hunting. You can write a hundred words about a guy stalking a deer or an elephant. It's not the same as being there. You have to experience it to understand it. You can't simply read it."

"I don't agree," I said boldly. "I'll never go deep water fishing, but your story was fascinating. I could picture it."

"Maybe..." he said quietly.

"So what *are* you writing?" I ventured.

He looked at his drink before answering, undoubtedly deciding how much he wanted to discuss his work. "I have a deadline for a collection of short stories. Max Perkins, my editor at Scribner, is pushing me hard."

I wondered how he managed writing every morning, fishing in the afternoon, and nightly drinking. The man's stamina was impressive.

"What about all of this?" I asked, raising my hands to take in the bar and Havana. "This town, the murders, Machado? That seems tailor-made for a novel."

Nodding, Hemingway said, "I have an idea I'm playing with. It takes place in Cuba and Key West. The protagonist—he's not a hero—has a boat like the *Anita*. He's a smuggler, like old Joe."

"And the struggle between the old man and fish—"

"Is nothing compared to the struggle between man and man."

"So, what's it about?"

Hemingway gave me a broad smile. "No, no, kid. You gotta buy the book. But it'll be a while."

My head was buzzing, and I vaguely wondered how many drinks I had consumed. Hemingway showed no signs of slowing down as we continued to talk and drink.

"Are you returning to Key West soon?" I asked, with a degree of self-interest. It would be a shame if he left Havana before I did.

Hemingway grimaced at the thought. "Soon," he said, "but there's still good fishing to be had."

"Then what? Write this smuggler's story?"

Hemingway's gaze shifted, his expression turning serious. "Not yet. There's something else I've always wanted to do, something that calls to me."

I raised an eyebrow, intrigued.

"A safari," Hemingway announced as if defying me to argue. "I'm going to Africa in the fall. It's the last place on earth where a man can feel alive."

"You mean kill," I dared to say.

Hemingway snorted at my *naivete*. Then, a hint of a cruel smile played on his lips. "In Africa, it's more than shooting some wild, dumb beast. There, it's a primal dance between man and nature, where simply surviving is the ultimate test. It's embracing the rawness of life, the thrill of the hunt. Kill or be killed. There's truth in that."

"Ever thought of owning your own boat?" I asked, shifting the conversation away from the intense direction it was taking.

"Of course. But, it's always better to have a friend who has a boat." He swirled the slush in his glass, thinking. "I might get one after the Africa trip. We'll see. Not sure what Pauline will think of it, though."

"Well, Ernest," I said, raising my glass with drunken camaraderie, "to fishing, writing, and the adventures awaiting. May they bring you inspiration and fulfillment."

"Call me Papa…"

"Papa," I said tentatively. It didn't feel right.

"Gentleman!" came a shout from the entrance. "I knew we'd find ya here."

It was de Castro and Phillips. Based on the volume of Phillips' voice, the Floridita was not their first stop this evening.

Phillips threw an arm across my shoulder. "We've been at Sloppy Joe's," he slurred. "When ya didn't show, we came to get ya instead. Both a ya. Papa! Yer comin' with us!"

"Oh?" Papa—Hemingway said dubiously.

"We are going to that special place you like," de Castro said, seemingly more in control of his faculties than his friend.

I was surprised to see de Castro. "I thought you had things to do this evening," I said, miffed that he had turned me down earlier.

"I do," he replied with a mysterious smile.

"Come on, Papa!" Phillips exclaimed. "It'll be an experience for young Evans."

Hemingway slid off his bar stool. "Yes," he said with a sly grin, succumbing to their enthusiasm. "It will be that."

Eleven

DE CASTRO SAID he was taking me far from the city, high in the surrounding hills, and centuries back in time. But first, we had to get out of Havana.

As we approached the Rio Almendares bridge, a barricade blocking the road forced us to halt. Two policemen stepped out of a small shack beside the road.

The shorter of the two strolled toward our car with an air of authority acquired from too many James Cagney movies.

"Say nothing," said de Castro. "We have the proper permits."

The policeman inspected the sheets of paper de Castro handed him with his flashlight, then shined his light on the three of us in the back seat. Without being asked, Hemingway and Phillips passed folded papers to the policeman. He scowled at me. I had nothing to offer him. Even my passport was in the hotel safe.

De Castro spoke in Spanish, and the policeman frowned. He returned the documents, stepped back from the car, and waved at his partner. The other man raised the pole and motioned for us to proceed.

As we drove away, I let out the breath I had been holding.

"It is nothing to worry about," Phillips reassured me. "Machado requires anyone leaving the city at night to have a permit. They are easily obtained—at a price. Everything in this country has a price."

My first thought upon seeing the police was our high level of alcohol consumption. However, that wasn't an issue with José's man behind the wheel.

"Why didn't the officer want to see my permit?" I asked.

Phillips chuckled, slapping me on the knee. "It's okay, amigo, you're with us! José convinced the cop that you're a tourist, lacking the necessary papers. You didn't see the pesos tucked into each of our permits. Like I said, you just have to pay!"

I looked at Hemingway for reassurance, and he gave me a knowing wink. I relaxed and admired the dark countryside.

We drove for twenty minutes, winding up a narrow dirt road that turned into a muddy, narrow trail. Eventually, we came to a clearing containing half a dozen cars of various ages and conditions parked in a row. De Castro's driver, Marco, waited in the car. I wondered why the bodyguard wasn't with us tonight.

At the edge of the opening, as if plucked straight from the primordial jungles of the Congo, sat a structure made of bamboo lattice and woven palm fronds. An intoxicating mixture of scents saturated the humid atmosphere; rum and lime mingled with the earthy perfume of sweat-slicked skin and rich tropical earth.

Inside was a bar and an open space of hard-packed dirt, which I assumed was intended as a stage. Three sinewy figures, faces obscured in shadow, crouched before large *ngoma* drums, calloused palms alternating between delicate finger-tapped rhythms and thunderous slaps. The frenzied pulsations of darkest Africa throbbed in a restless cadence that penetrated my brain.

Rickety chairs and a dozen warped wooden tables encircled the open floor area. Strings of bare bulbs dangled overhead, a feeble attempt at lighting that only heightened the primitive ambiance.

Dark Cubano faces inspected us as we found an empty table deep in the shadows. A heavy-set woman dressed in a floral tent placed a stoneware pitcher and four glasses on the table. Evidently, the choice of beverage was limited.

"You will like this," de Castro said, raising his glass. "It is a traditional drink called a *Canchánchara*."

He filled my glass, and we toasted. The heady concoction, white cane rum, honey, and lime juice, with hints of spice, coursed through my veins. Despite all the booze I had consumed that evening, I was not so much drunk as lost in myself, perhaps beyond drunk. The syncopated pounding of the *ngomas* vibrated in my bones, their frantic cadences blurring the sights and sounds into an intoxicating kaleidoscope of movement.

One memorable image still burns in my brain—Fela.

The drumbeats stopped suddenly, anticipation holding the assembled group of men in tense silence until the beaded curtain parted to unveil the statuesque, lithe form slinking toward us.

De Castro confided, "You will enjoy this. Señor Beals was quite taken by her dancing."

"Is this the rumba?" I asked.

"It is, and it is much more," de Castro smiled knowingly.

Fela was a towering ebony goddess adorned in a scrap of vibrant red linen knotted at her hips and a wisp of translucent fabric across the lush swell of bare breasts. Silver bangles encased one sleekly muscled arm, clinking with each languid movement. A behemoth of a man, well over six feet in height, bare-chested and glistening, launched into a furious tattoo on the double-headed *Batá* drum cradled in his lap.

At first, Fela remained motionless as that primitive beat began to take hold. Then, slowly, she began to move—each controlled sway and dip of her frame an overt invitation, an artfully choreographed seduction that completely captivated me.

I could scarcely breathe, utterly transfixed by the sinuous vision undulating mere feet away. Never had I witnessed such blatant, unabashed sensuality—my entire being focused on that lithe, glistening form as she surrendered herself to the rhythm.

Each roll of her shoulders and torso rippled like liquid shadows upon those sculpted contours. The rise and fall of her full breasts was almost hypnotic as rivulets of perspiration ran between their curves. Fela's lips parted slightly, forming silent words as if whispering an ancient spell in time to the pounding drums.

The staccato beat intensified to a fever pitch, the drummer's hands a blur of motion, sweat pouring from his straining muscles. Fela became fluid, spineless—transitioning from swaying undulations into a frenzied, trancelike whirling dervish.

Then, with a final explosive burst, the drums stopped. Fela arched backward in one searing spasm, every muscle pulled taut as a bow about to lose an arrow before crumpling in a boneless spiral at the center of the stage—chest heaving, lips parted, eyes closed.

"They don't have that in Kansas," Hemingway stated, taking a long drink and refilling his glass.

The four of us sat without moving, our senses overwrought. No one applauded, and I understood. What we had witnessed was more than sexual; it was spiritual, ancient, and dark. The musicians resumed their more sedate rhythm as the huge *Batá* player helped Fela off the floor. She appeared exhausted and tiny, supported by his massive arms.

De Castro looked at each of us and said, "I will be a moment. There is a man I must talk to."

Before anyone could comment, he rose from the table and circled the dance floor to the bar. I saw him engage a man in grey slacks and a long-sleeved guayabera leaning against the counter. As they spoke, the man looked over his shoulder at us.

Hemingway saw it and said, "So we are here under false pretenses," under his breath.

"What do you mean?" I asked, my mind still filled with images of Fela's body moving to the music.

"Apparently, we have come to this place for a clandestine meeting. I suppose the man at the bar is an informant of some kind."

"You've been reading too many novels," I scoffed. But, as I said it, a cloud of doubt entered my mind.

Turning his back on the men at the bar, Hemingway said, "So tell us, kid. What do you think of Cuban nightlife?"

"I'm overwhelmed," I replied truthfully. "I'll never forget what we just saw." I held my glass up to the feeble light. "Despite the best efforts of whatever this is!"

We shared a laugh, and Phillips poured another round.

"Tell me, Walker," he said, "all these photos you've been taking—what sort of story are you trying to tell? Do you think your pictures will add to Beals's book?"

I thought back to all the places I had been. The markets, the theaters, the street scenes. "To tell you the truth," I said slowly, "I'm not sure what story I'm trying to tell. So far, it's not the story Lippincott wants, I'm sure of that."

"What do you mean," Hemingway asked.

"I've got nothing better than most tourists take home to bore their friends," I hesitated, frustration building within me. "Except for the police arresting protesters at the Independence Day ceremony, they're not the kind of shots I expected from José…"

I trailed off, thinking about the last few days. While my frustration with José had been building, I could also recognize that it was partially my fault. After all, what would I choose to photograph, given a free rein? Would it be scenes of everyday life, of people struggling to survive? Would it be families waiting on breadlines or begging in the street?

No, my eye is drawn to the arch of a theater entrance, a wall postered over a dozen times, the sky sliced by the edge of a roofline, or the shadow of a Royal Palm cast on the sidewalk. The number of photos I had taken of a live human being could be counted on the fingers of one hand.

As if reading my thoughts, Hemingway said, "You know, Walker, if there's one thing I've learned as a writer, it's this: A good story is about the people. Not the place, not the action, not the drama unfolding—the *people*. Every story must have a conflict, whether love or war or life or death. And it's the people in that story who must experience the conflict." He raised a hand to indicate the building around us. "Cuba isn't the signs, the collapsing buildings, the storefronts, the balconies. That's not Cuba. Cuba is the people."

We were all moved by his passionate speech. It was something I needed to consider. I also needed to be more honest with myself. Why was I more drawn to capture the column's shadow than the beggar leaning against it?

The answer was self-evident: it was for the same reason I didn't sit before James Joyce at the Paris bookstore when presented with the opportunity of a lifetime.

I caught a furtive movement at the dimly lit bar from the corner of my eye. De Castro abruptly jerked his arm away from the grasp of the Cuban he was talking to. The man said something to de Castro, who replied angrily and stormed back to our table.

He didn't so much as glance at his vacant chair, hissing, "We go. Now."

Hemingway, who had observed the entire confrontation with narrowed, evaluating eyes, rose wordlessly from his seat, donned his fedora, and began moving toward the entrance. De Castro tossed a handful of bills onto the table's pockmarked surface before following us into the rain.

Far in the distance, lightning flashed over the ocean.

Inside the car, Phillips broke the silence. "A friend of yours?" he asked, his voice laced with sarcasm.

From his position in the front seat, de Castro spoke without turning his head. "I am sorry, my friends," he said with a stiffly clenched jaw. "I should not have brought you here. I needed to speak with this man about a story I am working on. He has information regarding the murder of the Valdez brothers."

"What had him so angry?" Phillips probed further.

The muscle jumped again in De Castro's taut jawline. "A matter of money. It was nothing."

The lie was transparent. De Castro was holding something back. No one spoke as Marco continued on the switchback descent toward Havana's lights, winking in the rain-swept valley below.

Then, Marco, whom I had never heard utter a single word, spoke rapidly in Spanish. De Castro spun in his seat, straining to see out the rear window. I was sandwiched between Hemingway and Phillips in the back seat and could see de Castro's tense expression illuminated by the following car's headlights.

As I began twisting for a better view, the pursuing car slammed into our left quarter. Metal shrieked against metal as we careened off the narrow road, churning through the sucking mud in a frantic, fishtailing arc. De Castro barked orders as our driver fought for control. Our vehicle regained the road and surged forward. The small wipers fought a losing battle against the rain pounding on the windshield. A blur of palm trees and dense foliage raced past on either side of the road.

"Who the hell have you pissed off?" Hemingway snarled at de Castro. He received no answer.

The car slewed around a sharp curve at breakneck speed, mud and water spraying behind us. Hemingway and I crushed Phillips against the door. My heart pounded in my chest. Who could have such murderous intentions? What had de Castro said or done to incite someone to ruthlessly run us off the road?

The sedan dropped back briefly, only to launch at us again, its headlights piercing the heavy rain.

Marco shouted, "*¡Espera!*" and yanked the steering wheel to the right. Our car slid in the mud and bounded over a ditch. A narrow path materialized before us, the thrashing palm fronds whipping the windshield as we rocked to an abrupt halt.

The pursuing sedan missed the turn. The car braked hard, the rear end fishtailing, before continuing down the hill. Its lights disappeared into the rain-soaked darkness.

"What the fuck was that?" Hemingway shouted, his angry words speaking for all of us.

De Castro twisted in his seat to face us, his expression a mixture of regret and anger. "I never believed they would be so reckless."

"They—whoever *they* were—were trying to kill us!" Phillips practically exploded, hands visibly trembling as he tapped out a cigarette.

"No," de Castro said flatly. "If they were trying to kill us, we would be dead." He took a deep breath and added, "Tonight, this was a warning."

Twelve

THE NEXT DAY, I accomplished nothing but moving slowly from one shadow to another. After our intense night in the hills, our desperate race in the rain, and our narrow escape from death, I found myself in no mood to venture beyond the comfort of the hotel.

Seated in the dark coolness of the lobby, I sipped iced tea and waited for the aspirin to ease my pounding head. My thoughts were consumed with questions as I replayed the previous night's events over and over in my mind.

The change in de Castro's demeanor after his conversation with the mysterious man at the bar left me confused. Something had transpired, something unexpected and unsettling. The man was not an informant. His demeanor and actions indicated he must hold a position of authority over de Castro. That much was clear, but what was their connection?

Interwoven with images of Fela's dance, I remembered Phillips' skepticism regarding the subject matter of my photographs. Why, amidst the daily violence that plagued Havana, was de Castro choosing to show me only the mundane façade of the city?

De Castro was keeping me at arm's length for an unknown reason. It puzzled me, for it seemed contradictory for a man like him—a man Beals described as driven by a genuine desire to expose the truth—to shield me from the crimes of Machado, the crimes of Cuba.

Was it a matter of trust? Did de Castro consider me unworthy of documenting the truth? Or was it a calculated move to shield me from the inevitable reprisal that would surely follow if I delved too deep?

My observations of de Castro's various clandestine meetings, his overly cautious navigation through the streets, and his relentless surveillance of any crowd had left an indelible impression on me. There was more to his reluctance than protecting me; that much I was certain. I couldn't shake the nagging feeling that he was more than a journalist—he had secrets of his own.

Then, Hemingway's speech about Cuba being its people echoed in my mind. As much as I resisted stepping out of my comfort zone, I knew I had a duty to fulfill. It was time to face the responsibility of my job, to uncover the Cuba Ernestine had hired me to find.

I made a firm resolution to confront de Castro, to discover the truth he was hiding, and to capture the reality of the people living with Machado's brutality.

Enough lurking in the shadows!

I was determined, though it took two days before an opportunity to confront de Castro presented itself. A message left at the hotel desk informed me he had urgent business to attend to, postponing our next meeting.

If de Castro was off on a secret mission, I would do what I could on my own.

Armed with my trusty reflex camera, I set out for the bustling Malecón the next morning. The boulevard teemed with activity, crowded by the presence of a passenger ship in for the day.

Everywhere I looked, sweating Americans photographed the superficial beauty of Havana, their pictures as mundane as those I had captured over the previous weeks.

It was maddening! I had to do better.

As the day unfolded and the sun rose higher overhead, I searched for the images I had missed before. It wasn't difficult. With renewed determination, I ventured deeper into the labyrinth of Old Havana.

Everywhere I looked, I found weathered faces that exposed a history of pain and suffering, while tired eyes held a deeply rooted determination. With each click of my shutter, I captured the essence of their struggles, the pressure of Machado's brutality, and the resilience that kept them fighting against all odds.

There were also those determined to rise above the oppression forced upon them. I secretly photographed a well-dressed woman waiting on the corner for a bus. She wore a crisp white linen dress, black pumps, and a matching clutch. A silk scarf adorned her neck, and her dark hair was tightly twisted in a bun.

She exuded an air of sophistication, and I tried to imagine her story. Was she a weary prostitute, ending a long night? Or perhaps a dutiful wife completing her shopping before heading home to prepare supper?

Continuing my walk, I arrived at a park filled with swaying Royal Palms and hydrangea-lined paths. Beneath the shade of the trees, I spotted a man asleep on a bench, his head propped on his hand, his legs stretched out before him. Was he resting before toiling in the fields or the factory? Perhaps he was a skilled cigar roller or a gardener tending to the marble palaces lining the Malecón.

I snapped roll after roll as I walked block after block. Here, a beggar sitting on the sidewalk, one foot bare, the other encased in a shoe so broken it needed to be tied together. There, a migrant family waiting for handouts at a breadline—the man with a baby on his hip, the woman pregnant, another child clinging to her hand.

Venturing into a deserted alley, I encountered a scene that broke my heart. A mother, perhaps a descendant of the original Cuban aborigines, the *Taino*, sat against an old wooden door. Her eyes were vacant and distant. In her arms, she cradled a toddler. Sprawled on the sidewalk slept a young girl no more than six. At her side, out to the world, was her brother, naked except for a filthy, tattered shirt. The children's bare feet were black and calloused from a life without shoes.

I discreetly captured several photos before the mother noticed my presence. Overwhelmed with emotion, I handed her two dollars, enough money to feed her family for a month. Tears welled in her eyes as she thanked me for the unexpected generosity.

Embarrassed at her reaction, I moved on.

And so my day continued until the sun cast a golden glow across the city. Exhausted as I was, I felt genuinely fulfilled. Finally, through the lens of my camera, I was uncovering the grit, the raw beauty, and the spirit of the Cuban people.

Each frame told a story of resilience in the face of tyranny. I believed the images I captured had the potential to drive change in this country—with or without Beals's book.

Machado had promised a democratic land of opportunity and plenty, and this was what he had delivered.

Now, it was my story to tell.

Passing by a Western Union office, it occurred to me I had not checked in with Ernestine since my arrival two weeks ago. By now, she must believe me abducted or murdered. I chuckled at the thought.

The tiny bell above the door rang merrily as I entered the cool office. The room had the familiar ambiance of every cable office I had ever encountered—with posters of various steamship companies adorning the walls and a mahogany counter holding a cash register and a stack of papers.

"I'll be right with you," a delightful British voice announced from behind a curtain. A young woman in her early twenties emerged. With bright green eyes framed by dark red hair and a sprinkle of freckles across her nose, the clerk was pretty in an Iowa farm-girl way.

"Hello," she greeted me, brushing a loose curl behind her ear. "How may I help you?"

In an instant, I was smitten.

"I, ah, need to send a telegram," I stammered.

"Well," said she with a hint of amusement dancing in her eyes, "you've come to the right place."

She pushed a notepad and pencil toward me. Trying to collect my suddenly scattered thoughts, I composed a short message to Ernestine: 'All well. Good pics. You will be pleased. E.'

The girl scanned my words and raised an eyebrow. "To New York, that's nine words at thirty cents and four periods at forty cents each." She tsked at my lack of economic sense. "You know, don't you, periods cost more? Change them to 'stop,' and you save forty cents! Also," she added, speaking as if to a schoolboy, "E is a word, so you might as well say who you are!"

Of course, I had sent telegrams before, but this young woman had thoroughly distracted me. I loved her delightful West London accent.

"Evans," I said, flashing a smile. "Walker Evans."

She extended her hand, and we shook. "Hello, Mr. Evans, I'm Dorothy, Dorothy Butcher." [16]

Briefly holding her hand, I noticed how small and delicate it felt in mine.

---

16 Nothing is known about Dorothy Butcher except that she was British and probably worked in the Western Union office. Evans mentions her briefly in his diary and a young woman standing next to Evans in a photo is believed to be her.

"I must say, Miss Butcher," I remarked, still holding her hand, "it's quite surprising to find an English girl working in a cable office in Cuba."

Dorothy withdrew her hand. "My father is at the British Embassy. I was rather bored and wanted something to do."

Observing the empty office, I raised an eyebrow. "And this is what you do for excitement? Send telegrams around the world?"

She laughed, the sound like delicate cymbals or the tinkling of crystal bells. With a teasing glint in her eyes, she said, "Well, I do meet the most interesting people. Sometimes, they use the money I save them to buy me a Coca-Cola."

I joined in her laughter. "Miss Butcher," I said, shifting to a more serious tone, "may I buy you a soda to express my gratitude for the fortune you saved me?"

"Seeing as how you are my first and only customer today, I think I can step out of the office for a short time. There's a delightful cantina nearby. And please, call me Dorothy."

She collected my four dollars and the telegram and disappeared behind the curtained doorway. I heard her speaking loudly to someone in the back room, then the rhythmic tapping of Morse Code. I pictured my words, transmitted as dots and dashes, traveling inside the underwater cable to Key West, then on to Miami, and eventually reaching New York. By the end of the day, Ernestine would be reading my cryptic note.

Dorothy emerged from behind the curtain, her smile radiant and infectious. She handed me my savings and said, "Shall we?"

Before the eruption of blood and death, Dorothy and I enjoyed a wonderful time together.

She led me to the small cantina on Cuba Street. We sat at a table on the sidewalk to capture the late afternoon breeze, and she ordered Coca-Cola for us both. The waiter provided glasses filled with ice without being asked. Dorothy said she came here often, and they took good care of her.

I did most of the talking, which wasn't hard with Dorothy. She listened intently to all I said, smiling radiantly, eyes wide with real interest. Her independence and intelligence reminded me of Jane Mason. In Dorothy, however, there was no evidence of the frenetic melancholy that hid behind Jane's beautiful face.

Our conversation flowed naturally as I described the photos I had taken earlier and the scenes' impact on me. As my focus shifted from architecture to living human subjects, I began to appreciate the immense suffering and misfortune that plagued this country. Despite all the rolls of film I had shot, the surface had only been scratched. There was so much more I needed to record.

Realizing I was talking far too much, I focused on Dorothy. "Tell me your story. What brought you to Havana? What does your father do at the embassy? Unless it's a secret!"

"No, he's not a spy! My father—"

And that is as far as she got.

The tranquil evening was shattered in an instant. A large sedan careened around the corner, its tires screeching on the cobblestones. A figure emerged from the rear window, a large barreled Tommy gun pointed directly at us.

Without thinking, I pushed Dorothy from her chair, our bodies hitting the sidewalk as a hail of gunfire erupted. In the same instance, I realized the target was not us but the two men sitting at the next table.

The deafening roar of the machine gun pierced the air. Chunks of bloody stucco exploded from the side of the building. The two men crashed backward, collapsing in a heap beneath their table.

Screams erupted from all directions as terrified patrons scrambled for cover. I grabbed Dorothy's arm and dragged her behind an arch in case that was not the end of the violence.

The assailants vanished as swiftly as they had arrived, their car disappearing at the next corner, leaving behind a trail of terror and confusion.

For a brief moment, the world stood still. Then, cautiously, heads emerged from hiding places, and the shaken customers ventured into the street to examine the carnage.

The twisted bodies of the two men lay entangled, their limbs contorted in unnatural angles, their clothing shredded. The amount of blood was appalling. Dorothy took one look at the bodies and turned away. Her face was pale, her lips quivered.

Taking Dorothy by the arm, we walked back to the Western Union office as fast as we could. A police siren wailed in the distance.

The telegraph operator met us at the door, his face etched with concern. Despite being hard of hearing, he knew something had happened. The man asked Dorothy a question in Spanish.

She looked down at her dress with a mixture of shock and horror, noticing the blood splatters for the first time, and burst into tears.

The old man took her in his arms, making soothing sounds a father might do for his daughter waking from a nightmare.

And a nightmare is what it was. I realized my entire body was vibrating despite not feeling particularly scared. I think everything had happened so fast that I was only now beginning to process it.

The man spoke again. Seeing my face, Dorothy forgot about her own troubles and led me to a chair. "Sit, Walker," she said as if I were a dog. She wiped away her tears and looked into my eyes. "Are you okay?" she asked, her voice filled with genuine concern.

I didn't seem capable of speech, so I took a deep breath and nodded. Soon, I stopped shaking, and a strangled laugh erupted from my throat.

"That was quite the first date," I said and laughed again, longer and harder. Dorothy studied my face and then burst out laughing as well. I'm sure the old man thought we had both lost our minds.

Thirteen

"I WANT TO KNOW what the hell is going on, José."

De Castro and I sat in the back of his sedan as Marco drove us south into the Cuban farmland. A cool morning breeze blew through the open windows, carrying the sweet smell of molasses. Cane fields crowded each side of the road, fading into the distance.

"I do not understand your comment," he said, but the way he avoided looking at me said differently. This morning's destination was a sugar processing plant near Quivicán, two hours south of Havana.

Turning to face him directly, I said, "José, you know what Beals was doing when he was here. You were with him most of the time. No one cares how sugar is refined. It is the same all over the world. It's hot and sticky. What Beals wants, what I want, is to show how the workers, those in the fields, those in the factory survive such hardships."

Still, José said nothing.

"What happened at the bar the other night?" I probed, attempting a different approach. "We could have been killed, José."

His jaw clenched, and I sensed the battle raging within him. Staring out the window, he finally spoke, his voice thick with emotion. "I am following orders, Walker. This is not what I wanted for you."

My voice firm, I demanded answers. "Orders? Whose orders, José?"

"The man I spoke to at the bar, he is my commander. I asked for a meeting to argue my case. To fight for you. That is why we drove up into the hills."

It was my turn to say, "I don't understand."

De Castro took a deep breath and looked directly at me. "Walker, I am a commander in the ABC."

My mouth fell open, the shock of José's words washing over me. Beals had explained that the ABC, the *Abecedarios*, had formed two years earlier from a wide spectrum of smaller factions. It was difficult to reconcile the man beside me, who had shown kindness and compassion, with the existence of a secret organization known for extreme violence, including bombings and assassinations.

I glanced at Marco, the ever-silent presence in the driver's seat.

De Castro answered the unspoken question. "Marco is a trusted member of my cell. We are both committed to the cause. No matter what the cost."

"No matter the cost?" I said slowly, struggling to control my growing anger. "No matter the cost? José, yesterday, two men were shot ten feet from me. Was that the work of the ABC?"

De Castro's eyes widened with genuine concern. "You were there?" His response answered my question.

"Yes," I said. "I was with a girl I met at the Western Union office. We were talking, having a soda, when a car passed by and machine-gunned those men. She was splattered with blood, José. Were they government officials of some kind?"

"Not really," he replied, shaking his head, "I am so sorry to hear this. Those men, they were *Porristas*. They tortured and murdered a member of another cell. At the bar, when my commander refused my request, he told me the B7 cell would soon carry out the hit."

I was becoming more confused by the minute. "What do you mean, B7? What is that, a code?"

"It is the designation of the cell. Each of the founders formed their own cells, and each cell has members who form other cells. We are forbidden from knowing the members of other cells.

We only know our commanders. Including Marco, I have four men working under me."

My mind returned to that perilous race down the rain-soaked mountain road. The ABC had involved me in two near-fatal incidents in quick succession. "We could have been killed on that road!" I shouted, my anger boiling over. "Was your commander willing to *kill* us?"

"No! The driver, he knew the car contained important *norteamericanos*. The ABC would not want the publicity. My commander, he wanted to remind me that we are all expendable, that we must obey orders regardless of the consequences."

The reckless disregard for our lives was maddening. "I refuse to accept that, José! We could have died. Your *commander* had no right to gamble with my life, with the lives of others. I am *not* part of this," I declared firmly.

De Castro raised a hand in a gesture encompassing the world around us. "Yet, you are here."

To avoid saying anything I would regret, I sat back in my seat and watched the rolling countryside. Tobacco and sugarcane fields stretched into the distance.

I sorted a hundred conflicting thoughts before I spoke again. "Explain to me why the ABC, an organization committed to overthrowing Machado, doesn't want me to document the suffering of your people. That's precisely why I came here—to provide photographic evidence for Beals's observations."

"Listen, Walker," José said, his voice low and urgent, "I cannot tell you everything. I can say this: Beals's book, the one about to be published, could jeopardize everything we are working for. The ABC, Welles, even Machado himself—they are all walking the tightrope of diplomacy. The book, it must not be published."

"But why?" I asked, my voice betraying my frustration. "Why would exposing the suffering of the people jeopardize the cause?"

De Castro smiled thinly, acknowledging that I had asked the right question. "The ABC is at the table, you Americans would say. Welles talks to our leaders, and it is clear the ABC, all the various factions for that matter, must ensure Machado has a way out. A way to not lose face, as the Chinese would say. Welles, he came here thinking he could re-establish order so American businesses could return to normal. He now understands Machado will never release his stranglehold on our people. Machado, he can play no role in Cuba's future, Walker. We believe Welles intends to have him replaced. If the world learns the truth about the man, and Machado has no safe place to go, he will refuse to give up his power and make things worse for all of us."

I absorbed his words, the complexities of the situation slowly sinking in. It was a delicate dance, a high-stakes game being played by all parties involved. The struggle for justice and freedom was far more intricate than I had imagined. The lines between friend and enemy are thin and often blurred.

'I don't think it is working," I replied. "Yesterday, two of his men were murdered in broad daylight. That isn't exactly reducing the violence."

"Those men, they had to die. It had been arranged days before. The one who pulled the trigger, he was the brother of the murdered man. He was allowed his revenge."

"It seems to me," I said slowly, realizing I risked alienating de Castro completely, "your ABC is no better than Machado's goons. Both seem exceptionally willing to murder for their cause."

De Castro spoke sharply. "You do not know. We fight for freedom. Machado fights for power and money—no matter the cost to Cuba."

"So why did you argue with your commander, José? Why is it I don't think you really believe what you are saying?" De Castro faced the window again, his chin resting on his fist. "You worked with Beals; you know what he is like. His passion is equal to yours in his own way. His book could be powerful enough to force Machado to leave Cuba, with or without a safe haven. Who cares where he ends up? Many people believe his book will make a difference to your country. Don't you?"

"Of course I do!" he spat. "But I have my orders!"

"From men willing to endanger your life and others just to send a message!"

We drove south in silence for several miles. Then de Castro abruptly sat forward and spoke sharply to his driver. I could see Marco studying his boss in the rearview mirror, and then he nodded curtly.

At the next intersection, he turned onto a dirt road, descending toward a small village in the distance.

"Where are we going?" I asked, realizing the road did not lead to a sugar mill.

De Castro's face was dark, his lips pulled tight. "I am giving you what you want," he said.

The rutted and dusty road ended abruptly as we reached the outskirts of a sprawling village. Our car, ill-suited for such terrain, struggled to navigate the rough path and was forced to stop on a rise. Further progress was impossible.

The road into the village resembled a dry wash, where torrential rains created a treacherous landscape of stagnant puddles, chunks of broken concrete, and rocks of various sizes. Two pigs wallowed in a large, murky pool of brown water. A grimy toddler clad in a homemade shirt, barely reaching his knees, stared at us wide-eyed.

The jumble of flimsy shacks lining the narrow, twisting street were haphazardly constructed using banana leaves and tree bark secured with rusted wire or twine. Their thatched roofs, made of grass or palm leaves, offered little protection from the elements. Some villagers had added a tin metal roof, a small sign of relative wealth.

I struggled to fathom how humans could live in such conditions. During my journey to the South Pacific islands, I observed modest native houses that were more substantially constructed than these.

"This village, you will find all over Cuba," de Castro said, waving his arm to indicate the houses below. "There are small towns, perhaps with blockhouses. This village, it is typical. The men from this village, they are cane cutters. Over the past year, half a million men lost their jobs. Those still employed have seen their wages plummet from a dollar fifty a day to only twenty-five cents. Other industries are organized, yet the sugar workers, they have been neglected by unions. No one cares about them."

We were drawing attention, and I wanted to document the scene before it was filled with people. I wanted a long shot, so I unpacked the large camera and set it on the tripod.

"Why use this camera?" de Castro inquired in an obvious attempt to restore normalcy. "Would your smaller camera not work as well?"

"For most of my pictures, yes, but not this shot," I explained, accepting his peace offering. Then, speaking from beneath the hood, I continued. "With the lens opening set at *f*64, I can achieve remarkable depth of field with exceptional detail. Also, the flexible bellows of this camera allows me to correct the distortion of the vanishing point and bring everything, from the foreground to the distant background, into sharp focus. It will be a great shot."

I carefully composed the frame and took four exposures, making minor adjustments to achieve perfection. We disassembled the equipment and secured it in the sedan's trunk when I was satisfied.

Three men, dressed in rough cotton shirts and pants, their faces shaded by large straw hats, walked up the hill toward us. De Castro met them halfway. Judging by his full white beard, the oldest among them greeted de Castro with a friendly handshake and a clap on the back. Apparently, they knew each other. Then, the two other men shook his hand.

I waited by the car while de Castro spoke to the men. At one point, he raised a hand in my direction. From their smiles, I gathered I was welcome to enter their village.

I retrieved my reflex camera and hurried to join de Castro and the three men. As I walked down the main street, faces peered from the shacks. Our presence was undoubtedly a rare occurrence, yet no one made any move to obstruct our progress.

When I joined de Castro, he said, "Walker, I wish to introduce my uncle, Eduardo Fernández de Castro Garrido. He has no English."

"Your uncle?" I asked, shaking hands with the three men. I missed the names of the other two as I tried to connect de Castro to this impoverished place.

De Castro raised both arms to encompass the village. "This is where I grew up," he said with a quick smile. "This is my village."

"And your parents?" I asked. "Do they also live here?"

Indicating the old man, de Castro said, "My parents, they died when I was five. My uncle and aunt raised me and my sister. They spent every *centavo* they had to ensure I received an education, riding the bus daily to the school in Quivicán.

"And you eventually attended Havana University?"

"When I was fourteen," de Castro continued, a spark of pride in his eyes, "I won a writing competition. My story was published in *The Havana Post*, and I was permitted to attend a boys' school in Havana. I did well and later studied journalism at *Universidad de La Habana.*"

I was utterly amazed by de Castro's journey, realizing that the man walking beside me had emerged from the depths of poverty to become a talented and educated individual. It was a testament to his resilience and the unwavering support of his uncle and aunt.

"You never told me any of this," I said.

"You never asked," he replied with a shrug.

We spent an hour in the village. I met de Castro's aunt and photographed her baking bread in an ancient brick oven. A bent back and gnarled fingers did not keep her from laboring all day in the oppressive heat of the bakery.

I believe I captured the real essence of the village in the pictures of children playing in the mud puddles. How many of them would go to the university, I wondered. For that matter, how many of them would live to adulthood?

More than the evident poverty, I was struck by how quiet it was in the village. There was no electricity, no running water, and no telephone service. Even the children played quietly. I felt as though I had stepped back in time a thousand years.

The photographs would please Beals and Lippincott. However, the growing question in my mind was: would Machado's Secret Police allow me to leave the country with such provocative images? The portrayal of abject poverty was a direct challenge to their narrative of a worker's paradise.

I considered de Castro's earlier comments regarding Machado's need to maintain a semblance of respectability in the eyes of the world. The photographs I had taken, coupled with Beals's book, clashed with the interests of my country's State Department, the Cuban government, *la Porra*, the ABC, and who knows what other factions.

Driving away, I expressed my gratitude to de Castro for guiding me to the village and acknowledging the risk he was now taking by disobeying his commander. I felt de Castro and I had entered a new phase in our relationship.

Perhaps a more dangerous one.

With that thought in mind, I checked Marco's face in the rearview mirror. He drove stoically, his jaw clenched. Where were his loyalties, I wondered.

Back on the main road, we continued south to the sugar refinery. I asked José what caused the sudden decline in wages he mentioned earlier.

"The price of sugar," de Castro said as if the answer were obvious. "For 250 years, sugar has been the lifeblood of Cuba's economy. Machado, he requires a great deal of money to sustain his power and lifestyle. At the request of your State Department, American banks have loaned him huge amounts of cash, effectively placing him under their control. As *colateral*—you say security— he allowed the sugar cartels to manipulate Cuba's sugar production in the global marketplace. In one year, our production has been cut in half, strangling us, while other countries increase production. In this way, the price of sugar is controlled."

I struggled to understand the intricacies of this advanced economics. "Cuba is one of the largest sugar producers in the world," I mused. "I would have assumed that it would be immune to fluctuations in the global market. With the right management, Cuba could control the price of sugar on their own terms. It could end this poverty."

"It is not so simple," he continued. "It is a vicious cycle. Machado, he relies on the United States to maintain his power. He is indebted to the banks, the sugar cartels, and the State Department. The more he appeases his masters, the more the people of Cuba suffer. And the more they suffer, the greater the risk of uprising from unions, students, and the wealthy who oppose Machado's regime. Cuba is on the brink of civil war. When it happens, thousands of acres of American-owned sugar cane will burn. Revolutionaries will smash the mills that have become symbols of their misery."

"Only worsening the situation," I sighed, overwhelmed by the complexity of the problem. "Is there any way out of this predicament?"

"Yes," de Castro stated with conviction. "The situation is *muy mala*, but the solution *es facil*, easy: Machado must leave the country. Or die."

Fourteen

DE CASTRO WAS A CHANGED MAN. It was as if a burden had lifted from his weary shoulders, leaving an unwavering sense of purpose behind. Such is often the state of a man who has chosen his path and accepted his fate.

His transformation was evident as we discussed the orders he had received from his ABC commander. The orders de Castro was now willing to defy.

As he had explained, the ABC and others negotiating with Ambassador Sumner Welles had agreed that casting a negative light on Machado and his regime would jeopardize the ongoing discussions. The world, they reasoned, must not turn its back on this monster, as it would leave Machado no refuge if it became necessary to forcefully remove him from power—a possibility growing more likely with each passing day.

I was genuinely pleased by de Castro's change of heart, although I couldn't ignore the increased threat to his safety and mine.

"This will create problems between you and your commander," I reminded him.

"It will," he replied with gallant composure. "Hopefully, you will be back in New York before they know what we have done. Regardless, Walker, I no longer care. What you are doing, it is important. We must show it to the world. Welles's negotiations will not produce a solution. Too many different groups are involved, each with their own vision for the future of our country. It will soon fall apart, and Machado, he will remain in power if we do not act."

His words lingered in my mind as we drove to the coal piers on the far corner of Havana harbor. De Castro insisted on showing me this operation. It was, he said, another example of Cuba's dependence on other nations. Through a combination of dwindling reserves and mismanagement, Cuba could no longer produce enough coal to satisfy the requirements of its own industries. As a result, large quantities of coal had to be imported from England and the United States.

We parked on the boulevard, collected my equipment, and walked onto the pier. The sky was dark blue and cloudless, the harbor jade green, rippled by a stiff ocean breeze. The entire pier was covered in a layer of black grime and spilled coal chunks that crunched beneath our feet. Grit blew in miniature tornadoes, instantly irritating my nose and eyes and sticking to my damp neck.

Fortunately, I had opted for the dark brown suit instead of my usual linen attire. I doubted my shirt would survive the day.

While my suit and body could be cleaned, I worried about my camera equipment. Dust, especially gritty particles, could ruin the delicate mechanism of the lens. Any photo I attempted would have to be sheltered, away from the relentless wind.

A three-hundred-foot collier ship dominated one side of the pier. Black streaks ran from the ship's deck, partially obscuring the rust and peeling paint on the hull.

As we approached, the ship's boom hoisted a large steel bucket from its hold, swung out over the pier, and dumped its contents—tons of coal—onto an ever-growing pile.

Amidst this chaotic activity, a dozen men toiled with flat-bladed shovels. Some worked feverishly to level the pile, preventing it from towering too high. Others strained to load the coal onto sturdy wagons. Two additional crews were engaged in similar tasks a hundred feet down the pier. I pictured more men laboring to load the buckets inside the ship's dark cargo hold.

All the men were caked in coal dust, making it impossible to determine the true color of their skin, a visual testament to the equality of their shared labor. Each wore some form of hat to protect them from the relentless sun and a sweat-stained bandana about their neck. Their tattered and soiled clothing blended into one predominant shade—black.

Among the workers, I spotted the former mathematics professor I had talked to at the cantina several days before. A wide grin spread across his weathered face as he recognized me, his white beard forming a stark contrast against his coal-blackened skin.

"You found us!" he said enthusiastically, shaking my hand with an iron grip. "I told my men how the American photographer and his friend confronted *la Porra* and lived!"

Amused at his exaggeration, I asked if his crew would consent to having their photo taken.

Trusting their foreman's judgment, the men eagerly consented. I positioned them against the warehouse's remarkably white stucco wall, emphasizing the striking contrast between their soot-covered bodies and the backdrop.

Every dust-filled pore, every vein, and bead of sweat showed in vivid detail through the camera lens. I could see the suffering and pain in their eyes, as well as the strength. I believe it was my best work to date. Hemingway would be pleased to know I had discovered what he called the real Cuba.

As I completed a series featuring the old man by himself, de Castro cleared his throat to get my attention.

Withdrawing my head from beneath the camera hood, I followed his gaze to the far end of the pier. Though I could not discern his face, there was no mistaking the figure of Colonel Antonio Jiménez, head of the Secret Police.

"How long has he been there," I asked, a knot of unease tightening in my gut.

"I spotted him earlier this morning when you were photographing the young *jinetera*. He remained in his car then but now has tailed us here. It would seem he wants to talk."

There was no way to avoid it. We would need to pass Jiménez to reach our waiting car. I folded the camera, stashing the lens back in my bag. Then, we thanked the old man, wished him well, and returned to the boulevard as casually as possible.

The head of Machado's Secret Police exuded an air of power and menace that could rival Al Capone. His bloodshot eyes reflected the darkness within his soul.

My stomach clenched tighter with each step we took.

"Good afternoon, *Coronel*," De Castro said without a trace of nerves. He spoke English for my benefit.

Jiménez remained silent, a smoldering cigar nestled between his thin lips. With practiced precision, he removed it from his mouth, expelling a cloud of smoke.

"I would hate to think you are interfering with our workers," Jiménez finally spoke, his deep voice rumbling with a slight lyrical accent.

De Castro offered a disarming smile, while his words displayed extraordinary bravery bordering on recklessness. "Rest assured, *Coronel*, we have caused no disruption. The colliers were merely taking a well-deserved break from their back-breaking labors."

Jiménez blew more smoke in our direction; his actions were deliberate and intended to irritate us. He examined the cigar closely before flicking the stub into the bay.

"Regardless," he growled, his voice seething with menace, "photographing buildings and statues is one thing. Capturing images of prostitutes and dock workers is an entirely different matter. I do not believe these people wished to have their pictures taken."

During this exchange, I stood silently, clutching my camera to my chest, probably resembling a guilty schoolboy caught stealing a pastry.

"They did not object, *Coronel*. In any case, we are finished," de Castro stated, attempting to move past Jiménez. My eyes darted to our driver, who stood behind the open car door, his arm subtly positioned at his side, perhaps concealing something. Could it be a gun?

"Where were you yesterday?" Jiménez barked suddenly, his voice demanding and cold.

De Castro hesitated a moment, then said, "We drove south. Señor Evans, he wished to visit a sugar refinery to document Cuba's thriving sugar industry."

Jiménez snorted dismissively. "Be aware," he warned, casually retrieving another cigar from his vest pocket, "we may be forced to inspect the *norteamericano's* photos before he departs our country. We do not want any industrial secrets exposed, do we?"

"I assure you, *Coronel*," De Castro scoffed, "we took no such photographs."

"See that you don't," Jiménez sneered, his eyes narrowing.

Naturally, de Castro couldn't resist the temptation to provoke Jiménez further. "And you be careful, *Coronel*," he taunted as Jiménez turned to walk away. The colonel paused, his back to us. De Castro continued, "I would hate to see you get coal dust on your suit."

My breath caught in my throat at de Castro's audacity. Mocking a man like Jiménez was a dangerous game. I didn't exhale until I was safely seated in the back of our car, the door firmly closed.

"What the hell was that!" I cried in disbelief as we drove away. "Are you out of your mind?" This newly liberated de Castro was proving dangerous.

"Yes," de Castro chuckled, "I am certainly out of my mind. Jiménez, he must not think he can intimidate us."

I barked a nervous laugh. "Well, I can tell you he did a damn good job of it. He is a killer, José. We shouldn't cross him."

"Walker," de Castro said, facing me directly, "you crossed Jiménez the moment you set foot on this island."

Fifteen

THE EVENING AIR WAS HEAVY with the threat of another storm. A haze of cigarette smoke and soft guitar music floated from the door as I entered the Floridita.

My eyes, adjusting to the dim interior, found Hemingway at his usual perch at the end of the bar. I hadn't seen him since the night of that wild race down the mountain.

It was relatively early; the nightly crush had yet to descend. A tired working girl, a handful of locals, and two American couples accounted for the patronage. I slid onto the stool next to Hemingway, saying hello.

"Where the hell ya been, kid? I've been drinking alone." Hemingway's gruff voice indicated he had been drinking for some time.

I chuckled at his remark. Someone always tried to spend a minute or two with Papa at his favorite haunt. The bartenders had perfected the art of gently shooting away the starstruck before they could make fools of themselves or, worse, irritate the great man.

A Daiquiri materialized before me, its frosty glass beading with condensation. I took a sip, feeling the icy chill stabbing my brain. The drink was exceedingly sour.

"This is different," I said, my mouth puckering.

"Huh," grunted Hemingway. "I'm trying something new. Constante's Daiquiris are too damn sweet. These are Number 3, made without sugar. What do ya think?"

"I think I'll stick with the old Number 3," I said, waving a hand to get a bartender's attention.

He took my drink and poured it into his glass, announcing, "I like it. I saw him add a few dashes from a bottle he has below the bar. Says it's his secret ingredient, and he'll stop serving me if I tell anyone." He paused, then whispered, "It's oil of lime."

I laughed and said, "The secret's safe with me. Maybe Constante should name it after you."

An eyebrow arched in agreement.

After a few sips of my restored drink, I said, "Well, you'll be happy to know I took your advice."

"My advice?" he scoffed. "I don't remember giving advice, kid. Learned long ago that no one listens. If it's worth knowing, you gotta discover it yourself."

"No," I countered, "you gave me good advice. Your exact words were: 'Cuba is the people.' I took it to heart and have been photographing faces and figures instead of factories and facades."

He groaned at my poor alliteration, although his interest was piqued. "Tell me what you've seen," he said, resting his chin on the palm of his hand, his forehead furrowed with anticipation.

"Well," I hesitated, delighted he was interested yet shy to describe my work, "I believe it is good. Just today, José led me to a street near Chinatown, which he said was the 'red-light' district."

"Ah," Hemingway said with a knowing smile. "And you maintain this was purely artistic pursuits?"

"Yes! I managed to capture some fascinating shots—yes, with their permission—of a woman behind a window grating watching the street, two lovely working girls washing their unmentionables in the courtyard…"

I trailed off, reflecting on the diverse and captivating faces I had encountered, from the sweet-faced prostitutes to the black-faced colliers. Each struggling to live under the thumb of an oppressive rule of a ruthless dictator. Each with their own story. I prayed my photographs would reveal their plight to the world.

"What is it?" Hemingway prodded, seeing the change in my face.

"I was just thinking," I said slowly, "how innocent those women are in the light of day. But when you see them at night on the street...Christ, they couldn't be more than fourteen."

Hemingway's face darkened. "It's a damned hard life," he agreed, his voice low and rough. "No doubt about it."

The weight of Cuba's beauty and brutality settled over us as we nursed our drinks, the Floridita slowly filling with the evening crowd.

"Any news on Jane?" I finally asked.

Hemingway exhaled sharply. "She's gone back to New York. Grant says they're gonna fuse four of her vertebrae. That's not good."

"Will she come back? After she recovers?"

The only answer was a tired shrug of his broad shoulders.

"The other day," I said, returning to our previous subject, "I photographed a man asleep on a park bench. I observed him for a while before I took his photo. I have to say, it made me wonder: Who is this man? What kind of life has he had?"

Hemingway scoffed dismissively. "A bum on a park bench is just that—a bum. You'll find them in every city. That's not unique to Havana."

"No, it's different here."

"How so?"

I thought for a minute before responding. "In Cuba, this man could have been anyone before his life was destroyed by Machado. He could have been a school teacher, like my new friend who works on the coal dock. I've seen these men when I go out early. You know how it is: early in the morning? Before the ice wagons come by with ice for the bars?"

Hemingway snorted. "That's damn poetic, kid. Maybe you should be the writer, and I'll take the pictures."

"No," I said firmly. "I tried being a writer. The camera's my voice."

He gave me a funny look but didn't comment.

"Oh," I added, almost as an afterthought, "and I met a girl!"

"Ha!" he barked, "So you *are* interested in women!"

Heat rose in my face, unsure if he was jesting or not. What had I done to warrant such a remark?

I had been very careful.

"Yes…" I replied evenly. "I like women. I met her at the Western Union office. We almost got killed having a soda."

"What?" Hemingway straightened on his stool, instantly alert. "How the hell did that happen?"

Before I could explain my cryptic remark, de Castro and Phillips joined us. They seemed to be a regular pair. When one appeared, the other was not far behind. As had become our habit, we moved to a table near the back of the bar.

Prompted by Hemingway, I entertained the group with the story of Dorothy and our brush with death. Despite the horror and danger I described, their laughter mingled with the clinking of glasses while toasting my chivalry.

Good company and good rum lifted my spirits. The dangers lurking in Havana's shadows seemed distant, momentarily held at bay by the warm glow of friendship and alcohol.

Then, De Castro's mention of our encounter with Jiménez sent a chill through our group. Everyone knew the horrors that man was capable of.

Phillips shook his head gravely. "That's bad news, Walker. Jiménez knows his life depends on Machado remaining in power. They're all getting nervous. Word is, Welles is already making noise about replacing Machado. The US has lost control of their man. Time to cut our losses."

"Do you think Jiménez will come after me? Try to confiscate my photos?" I asked the group in general.

Phillips drained his glass and raised it to the bartender. "He has the power to do it, my friend. His job is to keep Machado in power. He won't let you or Beals's book stand in his way. Question is, does he have the time to do anything."

"If Walker's already on his radar," Hemingway asserted, "he'll make the time. Jiménez is a loose cannon. While he might be Machado's dog, he also has his own agenda. When Machado falls, he intends to be the last man standing." He fixed me with a hard stare. "As in all great endeavors, the reward must be worth the risk."

"I agree," Phillips added. "Both Welles and Jiménez have reasons to keep your pictures from leaving the country."

"It may be too late," I sighed and then described the pictures I had taken recently: the gritty reality of poverty-stricken cane cutters and their miserable village, the depressingly young prostitutes, and weary colliers on the pier. "My subject matter is already controversial."

I didn't mention de Castro's change of loyalty or his association with the ABC, and no one had a reason to question it.

Phillips's voice rose. "It's not enough!"

"Why not?" I snapped. His drunken comment made me mad. How could he judge my work without seeing it? My photographs had caught the attention of Jiménez, for heaven's sake.

Phillips pointed a finger at me, eyes blazing. "If you wanna take pictures back to Beals, pictures that'll make a difference, that'll really matter, you gotta go to the *Diario* morgue. There are photos there, my friend, that'll make all the others seem trivial by comparison."

A newspaper morgue is a vast collection of back issues, rough notes, faded photos, and dusty evidence tucked away in basement vaults. At big city newspapers, the morgue is often guarded by a stern librarian or curator. In most cases, however, a journalist, or more likely a junior reporter, must search through years of files to locate some arcane item.

I shook my head. "I don't understand. What is in the morgue that could be that important?"

Phillips spoke in a hushed whisper, forcing us to move closer. I am sure we resembled conspirators planning the overthrow of the government...

"Last month," Phillips said, "when everything started going to hell, my wife, Ruby, and I were on our balcony. We heard shouting on the street. A boy ran toward us. He was alone in the street, weaving wildly from side to side as if he didn't know where he was. Then he stopped, raised his arms, and waved them wildly as he shouted, '¡*No tire mas, no tire mas!*' Don't shoot!

"Several men on the embankment above us appeared with rifles. They were waiting for the boy.

The first volley struck him in the back. He stumbled but did not fall. The second volley smashed into his head and shoulders. He collapsed in front of the statue of President Gomez."

"How can they get away with such an obvious crime," I asked, horrified by Phillip's story yet sure that such a thing was possible in Machado's Cuba.

"It's called *Ley de Fuga*. Literally 'law of escapes.' It allows for prisoners trying to escape to be killed. Legally."

I had no response. Hemingway growled deep in his throat like a lion sensing its prey. De Castro was clearly alarmed, though not because of the story.

Phillips continued. "The boy's body lay in the street for hours before anyone bothered to remove it. Long enough for a photographer to take pictures. The *Diario* never ran them. Machado threatened to shut down the paper. They're in the morgue. And there's more like it. Many more. After I wrote an article for the *Times*, I got death threats. Ruby and I had to cool our heels at the home of the Consul General for three days." [17]

Phillips sat back and took a drink from his fresh Daiquiri. When he spoke again, his slow

---

[17] Taken from J. D. Phillips, New York Times, 15 April 1933, Killing by Police of Cuba Witnessed by Correspondent

voice was thick with emotion. "The boy was fifteen, and on that day, his brother met the same fate. If Beals wants you to capture the Cuba he is writing about, you need those photos. That, my friend, is the real Cuba."

"*¡Ni pensarlo!*" de Castro gasped, waving a hand to stop Phillips from saying more. "Phil, it is too dangerous. I cannot take Walker to the morgue."

"You must!" Phillips slammed his hand on the table, startling everyone within earshot. "It's the only way to expose the truth."

Hemingway, who had been uncharacteristically quiet during this exchange, suddenly grinned. "I say we all go," he declared. "It'll be an adventure!"

That stopped the conversation in its tracks. I feared Hemingway's Daiquiri count had reached a record level.

"What?" de Castro choked. "Papa, you don't know what you are saying!"

"Yes!" Phillips shouted enthusiastically. "We'll all go!"

Hemingway rose from his seat, appearing sober and strong. "Follow me, men!" he bellowed. "We have a mission!"

I laughed at his uncanny Teddy Roosevelt impression. Then he looked at me. "Do you have your camera, soldier?"

"Always," I said, patting my coat pocket.

"Then we're off!"

Not sure what we were getting into, I followed Hemingway and Phillips as they marched out the door, leaving a bar full of bewildered patrons.

Behind us, de Castro begged, "Wait! We must not do this!"

And then he followed us into the street.

Sixteen

WE COULD HAVE WALKED from the Floridita to the *Diario* building, but de Castro's car was conveniently parked outside. After a night of drinking, the thought of stumbling the distance on foot did not appeal.

Marco parked the car on Teniente Rey near the side entrance of the newspaper office. A light rain dampened the pavement, the stones reflecting the streetlights in a hazy glow. Over the ocean, lightning foretold of worse weather to come.

De Castro, now sobered by the gravity of the risk he was taking, tried unsuccessfully to hush Hemingway, who was making a running commentary of our actions as if planning his next book. Perhaps this was a fool's errand.

"Papa, please lower your voice!" de Castro hissed. "I must enter the front door. You wait here. I will open this door from the inside."

We all indicated our agreement. Hemingway grinned. He was having far too much fun. De Castro sighed, a mix of resignation and apprehension, then headed for the main entrance. A newspaper never sleeps, and he knew the door would be unlocked. All he had to do was avoid any prying eyes.

As the three of us waited silently under the protective arch, Hemingway moved beside me.

"Listen, kid," he whispered, his voice steady and serious. "If you're concerned that Jiménez might seize your photographs, give them to me. I can take them back to Key West when I go in a couple weeks. I'll mail them to you in New York. Nobody pays any attention to me anymore. I come and go as I please."

I appreciated the practicality of his suggestion. "I would have to make prints and give you those," I said, thinking out loud. "The film, the negatives, those I must keep, regardless."

"Whatever you think best. I'll do my part."

"Thank you, Papa," I said, gratitude washing over me. Hemingway had suggested a solution before I had considered the problem. Come what may, we had a plan, and that felt good.

It seemed we waited for an eternity for de Castro's return. A car passed, its headlights momentarily blinding us. We pressed ourselves against the large door, deep in the shadows, and the driver continued without noticing us.

Finally, the lock clicked behind us, and the door swung open. De Castro held a flashlight, illuminating our faces.

"This is *not* a good idea," he stated for the record, then disappeared into the building.

The three of us navigated the dark hallway in single file. The smell of ink and machine oil permeated the air. The distant sound of typing echoed in the building, a reminder that we were not alone.

Eventually, we came to a narrow, descending staircase. De Castro's flashlight struggled to penetrate the stygian darkness.

"Fear not," Hemingway commanded. "I will remain here and guard the pass in case someone investigates."

And do what, I wondered.

We descended cautiously, keeping close to the small circle of light. Cool air carrying the ripe smell of mushrooms invaded our senses. I couldn't get rid of the idea that we were entering an ancient crypt.

"Be careful," de Castro breathed. "Here is the floor."

His flashlight illuminated a brick-lined hallway, its ceiling vaulted and foreboding. Support arches crossed the hall at ten-foot intervals, adding to the crypt-like atmosphere. Cobwebs clung to the corners. Bella Lugosi could have been lurking in the shadows.

Silently, we made our way to the end of the hall, the sound of our footsteps muffled by the dusty brick floor. The squeal of old hinges ruptured the silence as De Castro pushed open a heavy steel door. Beyond was a room crowded with old wooden filing cabinets. The musty air was heavy with the smell of aged newsprint and tobacco. A single desk with a green-shaded lamp stood in the center of the room.

Phillips pulled a chain, and a small pool of light illuminated the desk. The rest of the room disappeared in deep shadows. He then grasped the brass handle of one cabinet and yanked the drawer open, revealing a mass of loose papers and accordion folders.

"How do you know where to look?" I asked.

"I've spent hours down here," he replied, carrying a folder to the desk. We gathered closer to the circle of light. "Any journalist with credentials can use the morgue," he continued. "Since no one works here, I've been free to search for evidence. This file is a compilation of different sources. Until now, I haven't figured out how to get them out."

De Castro scoffed at Phillips' anxiety. "If you are found with these photos, they will ask you to leave. If I am caught, I will lose my job. Maybe my life."

"I'm sorry, José," Phillips said in a softer tone. "I know you're risking a great deal. Trust me, it's worth it."

He upended a folder, and a dozen black and white photos cascaded onto the desk. The first on the top of the stack took my breath away. A young man's battered and bloody face turned toward the camera. The photo had no artistry—its sole purpose was to document the man's death.

"This picture was the first I found," Phillips explained. "Last year, a story appeared in *El Pais* with a headline proclaiming: 'Death by Shooting of 17-year-old Gonzalez Rubiera Youth, Suffering from the Application of the *Ley de Fuga*.' With it, they published this image of the young man's lifeless body."

I picked up the picture and held it to the light. The young man's delicate features, almost feminine, belied the brutality he had endured. He could have been asleep except for the bruises and the blood running from the corner of his mouth.

"Tell him what happened to the editor," de Castro urged.

"Enrique Pizzi Porras, the night city editor of Havana's *El Pais*, waited for the first copies to roll off the press, wished his staff a Happy New Year, and walked across town to the sanctuary of the Mexican Embassy. He hasn't been seen since."

Phillips sorted through the stack and flipped a post-mortem photo of a man into the light. The gruesome image had a note attached that read: ABC killed by revolutionaries for being a stool pigeon, or 'long tongue.'

"This photo demonstrates that the brutality we witness is not limited to Machado," Phillips said, glancing at de Castro.

"This *brutality*," de Castro hissed, anger tightening his voice, "exists *because* of Machado."

Only I knew his reason for defending the ABC.

Phillips refused to engage in an argument. Instead, he continued to select more photos, revealing shocking images of a dead man lying on the street, surrounded by police, another man draped over the curb, and a young black boy inexplicably posed with a rope and a knife. The sight was distressing, assaulting our senses with a stark reminder of the violence that plagued the country.

"Enough," I moaned. "These are enough."

I adjusted the lamp and moved a high-back wooden chair against the desk. Bracing my arms on the backrest, I took two shots of each photo as Phillips placed them under the light, one after the other.

When I straightened and stretched my back, Phillips asked, "Good enough?"

I sighed deeply, emotionally drained by what I had seen. "This is more than we need to expose the truth."

"Then, we go!" de Castro announced with a sense of urgency. He was now defying his newspaper, the ABC, and Machado. His life was truly on the line.

We retraced our steps to the staircase. And there, waiting patiently in the darkness, stood Hemingway. He reached out, his hand firmly grasping the back of my neck as he asked, "Did you get what you came for?"

"Yes," I murmured. Now was not the time to describe the horrors I had seen.

De Castro pushed open the door and stepped out onto the covered sidewalk. A mix of frustration and disbelief escaped his lips.

"¡Coño!" he swore.

We joined him under the arches. A steady rain was falling, dissipating the light fog drifting in the empty street.

Our car was gone.

Seventeen

"Why would Marco leave us?" Phillips' voice trembled with a mix of confusion and fear.

De Castro's jaw tightened, and his eyes scanned the street in each direction, but he offered no reply. Phillips's words gave voice to the confusion and fear that gripped us all.

A brilliant flash of lightning split the northern sky, followed by a crash of thunder that shook the ground beneath our feet. In an instant, sheets of heavy rain cascaded down the narrow street, the deluge as sudden as it was fierce.

"We can't stay here," Hemingway's commanding voice broke the spell as he stepped out from the meager shelter of the archway. His thin cotton guayabera instantly became transparent, revealing a patch of dark chest hair. "We should go back to the Floridita. He's probably waiting there for us."

"Why would he leave us?" Phillips repeated.

"I'm sure he had a good reason," Hemingway replied. He grasped Phillips by the arm. "Come on, Phil. A little rain won't hurt you."

With that, the author marched resolutely into the storm. I caught a glimpse of de Castro's face, his eyes betraying his concern. He knew his driver—a man who had proven himself repeatedly—would never abandon us without a dire reason.

Something was very wrong; that much was certain.

My hand pressed against the camera buried within the folds of my coat pocket. I had to keep the camera dry and the film safe. Was I already placing my life in jeopardy by simply possessing these pictures? How far was I willing to go, I asked myself. I couldn't answer. Knowing these images held the power to shake Machado's regime to its core filled me with a purpose I had never felt before.

By the time we turned left onto Avenida Bélgica, we were all drenched to the bone, our clothes and hair plastered to our skin by the relentless downpour.

The wide boulevard, bustling with life during the day, was now empty and cloaked in deep shadow. Storefronts and cafés were shuttered and dark.

Over the sound of the rain, the roar of an engine caused us all to turn in alarm. Headlights pierced through the deluge, catching us in the intense beams like the proverbial deer.

De Castro muttered under his breath, his face etched with fear. "Go that way!" he hissed, pointing to a dark side street.

Hemingway immediately understood the threat. "Split up!" he shouted.

I stood rooted in disbelief, struggling to comprehend the unfolding chaos. Hemingway and Phillips vanished into the rain, each heading in a different direction. De Castro seized my arm, pulling me into the alley he had indicated. "We go!" he hissed.

My heart pounded as we sprinted along the narrow, unlit alley. The darkness enveloped us, making it impossible to discern our surroundings. Rain cascaded from the rooftops, filling the street. Each step sent water splashing, and my feet skidded on the slick cobblestones.

The intermittent flashes of lightning shattered the darkness, momentarily revealing our path before plunging us back into the consuming darkness.

"Who is it?" I gasped.

Between ragged breaths, de Castro said, "It is Jiménez! I recognize his car."

My mind reeled as the gravity of the situation began to take hold. How could Jiménez know we were at the newspaper office? More importantly, what was his intent?

At the next corner, de Castro abruptly turned me to the right. "Go to your hotel. I will find you later."

I hesitated, unwilling to go on without him. My eyes darted between the direction he pointed and the approaching car.

"Go!" de Castro's urgent voice jolted me from indecision. And with that, he sprinted in the opposite direction, disappearing into the night.

Casting one last fearful look at the approaching vehicle, I forced myself to move forward, my pace quickening with each step. The darkness of the street seemed to deepen as I ran, shielded from the car's headlights. I dared not look back.

Without warning, the sharp crack of a gunshot echoed in the street. I gasped in alarm, stumbled, and fell to my knees. A second shot, then another ringing out in rapid succession.

Then, an eerie silence settled upon the deserted streets, broken only by the rain splattering against the cobblestones.

I have no memory of finding my hotel. It was simply there, the sign above the door beckoning weary travelers.

I staggered up the steps, a disheveled, soaking mess, my soggy suit clinging to my frame. Sloshing steps echoed through the lobby as I approached the elevator.

The night manager rushed from behind the front desk, fear clear on his face.

"Señor Evans!" he cried. "Are you alright?"

"I'm fine, Alfredo," I said without stopping. Pulling the elevator grating closed, I said, "Please send the boy for my suit. It needs to be dried and pressed."

Alfredo stared with wide eyes. "*¡Si, señor!* Right away."

Safe in my room, I peeled off my clothes, leaving them in a soggy pile on the tile floor. Then I got a towel and stood naked in the bathroom, methodically drying my camera.

I must have been in shock. My mind slowly began to process the evening's events. What the hell had happened out there? The gunshots, the chaos—had Jiménez shot de Castro? Was de Castro lying on the cobblestones as his blood washed into the gutter?

And what had happened to de Castro's driver, Marco? Every day we had been together, the man was steadfast and silent. Perhaps he had driven to safety when he spotted Jiménez.

One of the horrible images I had copied this evening flashed in my mind's eye. It was a man killed by the ABC because he had betrayed his own people. Long-tongued, the sign read.

Perhaps it wasn't Jiménez who pursued us, but a member of de Castro's own ABC. Marco knew everything we did and was a member himself. Was his sense of loyalty to the ABC greater than to de Castro?

I didn't know what to think.

A sharp rap on the door made me jump. I wrapped a towel around my waist and opened the door with no small amount of trepidation. It was the boy sent to retrieve my saturated suit.

To my great relief, he held a cup of steaming coffee. I retrieved a peso coin from my dresser and thanked him. The boy grinned widely, appreciative of such a generous tip, and promised to return my suit by noon.

Noon would be about right, for I intended to sleep until then. Warmed by the coffee, I fell upon my bed, exhaustion overcoming my fear and concern for de Castro.

I would deal with it as soon as I…

Eighteen

STEAM ROSE FROM HAVANA as the city baked in the hot morning sunlight.

I slept deeply for several hours, but my mind began replaying the events of the evening over and over—the gunshots, the eerie silence that followed, and the desperate feeling of not knowing. With the sun shining through the cracks in the window, I abandoned any notion of rest, instead focusing on finding de Castro and protecting my photos.

I donned my freshly pressed suit, placed the all-important film rolls and plates in my valise, locked my room, and stepped out into the muggy streets. At the corner, I hailed a taxi. My destination was the Diario office, back to the scene of the crime.

The boy at the front desk knew nothing, so I asked to speak to Editor Diaz, whose name de Castro had mentioned several times. Even though he knew de Castro had been my escort in Havana, I needed to guard how much I divulged.

The news was grim. De Castro had failed to report to work that morning, his whereabouts unknown. His car and driver were nowhere to be found.

"Something happened here last night, Señor Evans," Diaz said as I prepared to leave. "A man who lives on the streets came to see me this morning. He claimed to see a man shot last night. The victim was thrown into a car and taken away." He peered at me over the rims of his half-moon reading glasses. "A shooting in Havana is hardly news. However, it would be unusual for Colonel Jiménez himself to be involved. I don't suppose you know anything about that?"

My face betrayed nothing, though my blood ran cold. For a fleeting moment, I debated confiding in the fastidious little editor, sharing the details of our encounter with Jiménez. Could I trust him? The tentacles of the ABC's reach were far and insidious. Caution was the prudent course.

If de Castro had been killed, wouldn't Jiménez have left the body in the street, a grim message to any who dared defy him? I, therefore, intended to work under the assumption that de Castro was alive. The question was: where would he be taken?

"No," I replied evenly. "From what I've seen, I have to agree with you. It sounds like a typical night in Havana. I left José at the Floridita, talking to Hemingway, and returned to my hotel. Why would you think it was José who was shot?"

"It is not like him to disappear," the editor explained. "He has been on Jiménez's watch list since your friend Beals came here last year."

"Why would Jiménez shoot him? It makes no sense."

"I don't know," he said, raising both hands in supplication. I knew he was lying.

"José told me Jiménez's men were always tailing us," I added, "but I rarely saw them. If it was José, and he was seriously injured, would Jiménez take him to a hospital?"

The editor snorted, his lips curling into a mirthless sneer. "That bastard would not care how badly hurt José was. If it was José, and if he is alive, he is in a cell at the police headquarters. We can do nothing."

The words hung between us, their finality sending a chill down my spine. "Have you attempted to find him?" I asked sharply, unable to mask my anger with the man's apathy. "Have you made any calls? Gone to the police?"

Diaz's face reddened. "You know nothing, Señor Evans," he spat. "If Jiménez had a reason to hold José, the police will do nothing. They work hand in hand with *la Porra*. And there is nothing we can do about it. Not without endangering our own lives. So it is in Cuba."

"Well, I'm not giving up," I said with as much bravado as I could muster.

Diaz studied me over the tops of his glasses. Then he shook his head. "Then I wish you good luck, señor. Now, if you will excuse me?"

I felt a mix of anger and determination coursing through me as the editor returned to his office, firmly closing the door behind him.

His attitude was infuriating—he and de Castro were most likely both members of the ABC, working together to undermine Machado. And yet, he was unwilling to become involved, despite knowing full well the danger de Castro was in.

I refused to accept that there was nothing to be done. There were people in this town more powerful than Jiménez and his goons, forces that could locate de Castro if properly motivated. And I had an idea how to contact them.

My next stop was the Western Union office.

Dorothy Butcher greeted me with a smile that instantly lifted the weight from my shoulders.

"I didn't know if I would ever see you again," she scolded playfully, her green eyes sparkling.

She came from behind the desk and placed a chaste kiss on my cheek. It caught me off guard, and a warm blush crept up my neck.

"I, uh," I stumbled over my words, my throat suddenly dry. "I have been very busy, you see. And I'm afraid I'm in a bit of trouble. Or, rather, my friend is."

A flicker of concern furrowed her forehead. "Your friend? Ernest Hemingway?" she asked. I had told her of my newfound friendship with the renowned author the afternoon we enjoyed sodas together. At the time, I was pleased that I could impress her.

Then...the blood and death.

"No," I said, shaking my head. "Although he did play a part in it."

Dorothy's anxiety grew, her eyes narrowing. "Part in what, Walker? What has happened?"

"A great deal," I signed heavily, the weight returning. "My guide, José de Castro, has been captured by the Secret Police. And he's been shot. I'm in danger, as well. Dorothy, I hate to ask, but I need your help."

She guided me to a chair and then perched on the edge of the desk. "Tell me everything," she urged, her voice a soft whisper.

So, I told her everything. We talked in hushed voices even though the old telegraph operator in the back room was nearly deaf.

I described the photos I had taken of the cane cutters, the prostitutes, the breadlines, and the dock workers. Then, without details, I described the images I had copied in the bowels of the newspaper office and our escape from Jiménez. And the gunshots. I omitted all references to de Castro's affiliation with the ABC.

Dorothy's beautiful eyes grew larger the longer I talked.

I finished relating my aggravating encounter with the newspaper editor and fell silent, awaiting her response. She stared at me for a moment before calmly asking, "What can I do?"

My heart swelled with gratitude. "I need to speak with the US Ambassador, Sumner Welles," I explained, outlining my half-formed plan. "If anyone can exert pressure on Jiménez, or Machado for that matter, it is he. But I can't simply walk into his office and request a meeting…"

I hesitated, my hand boldly reaching out to touch hers. "Do you think your father could speak with your ambassador? Perhaps the ambassador could request a meeting with Welles for me? Put in a good word, so to speak…"

Then, the enormity of what I was asking overwhelmed me, and I backtracked. "I know it's asking a great deal. It is too much, I'm sorry. I'll think of something else."

Dorothy looked down at my hand resting on hers. Embarrassed by my own forwardness, I started to pull away. She turned her hand over and grasped mine. Her hand was warm and soft.

"Of course, I'll ask, Walker," she said with determination. "This is serious, and we must act swiftly!"

We?

"No, I can't ask you to get involved in this," I protested.

"What do you think you just did?" she chided gently. "Let me see if I can reach my father. He is often in a meeting.'

I realized Dorothy had never divulged her father's role at the British Embassy. We were rudely interrupted by a gunman before she could describe his job.

"You never told me," I said, "what your father does? I only know he's not a spy."

She tilted her head. "Didn't I? Well, he is the Minister Plenipotentiary."

My face reflected my confusion.

"My father, Walker, is Sir John Butcher, His Majesty's Ambassador to the Republic of Cuba. I think he can arrange your meeting."

Nineteen

"FATHER IS AT HOME," Dorothy informed me after a short phone call, her tone clipped, recognizing the urgency. "He's not been feeling well the past few days."

"Nothing serious, I hope."

Her reply was a slight tilt of her head. I didn't dig deeper.

Lady Dorothy, as I now thought of her, said the family had relocated here from Washington two years earlier. However, their time in Cuba was to be short-lived, as Sir John had recently been appointed Ambassador to Argentina. They would leave within the year.

"I'm not a Lady," Dorthy admonished when I called her one the second time. "My father was appointed to the Order of the British Empire. It doesn't confer anything on his children."

"Oh, I'm so disappointed!" I teased, earning a punch on the arm.

To say I was shocked to learn Dorothy's father was the British ambassador would be an understatement. My mind was churning on the possibilities of this meeting. What could I reveal about de Castro's dire straits without further jeopardizing his safety? What if her father *could* arrange a meeting for me with Ambassador Welles? Would Welles be willing to help?

I took a deep breath. One step at a time.

The narrow, tree-lined streets and colorful colonial facades gave way to the opulent grandeur of the British ambassador's home, a masterpiece of Victorian splendor. A sweeping drive curved past meticulously manicured gardens, leading to the grand entrance.

The taxi dropped us at the front door, and we entered the house as if we lived there. Admiring the high ceiling of the foyer, I had to ask, "Why would the ambassador's daughter want to spend time at a Western Union office?"

My question elicited a frown. "You mean, why aren't I spending my time at garden parties and political functions like my mother instead of grubbing away at an actual job?"

"Well..."

"Opportunities are limited, Walker," she continued, head tilted to the side. A very becoming flush had risen on her neck. "I want to be in the city, get to know the people, and be part of Cuban life. The telegraph office is a safe place to work that also allows me some freedom."

She fixed me with a challenging stare, daring me to question her, then continued into the house.

Sir John was enjoying a late breakfast in the glass-walled conservatory. Large ferns and potted palms crowded the room. It was pleasantly warm and humid. The air was thick with the heady scents of exotic blooms and rich, loamy earth, a fragrance at once intoxicating and soothing.

As we entered, the ambassador rose from his seat, brushing a kiss against his daughter's cheek before extending his hand in greeting. It was evident from that first that Sir John was unwell—his skin bore an almost translucent pallor, untouched by the tropical sun. [18]

"You must be the young man my daughter keeps talking about," were his first words.

"Father!" cried Dorothy, and we both blushed.

Chuckling at our discomfort, Sir John gestured for us to take our seats. "Do you care for lunch, Mr. Evans? Afraid it's only dippy eggs and soldiers—a bit of comfort food this morning, what?"

I started to decline but was interrupted by Sir John's shout for a servant. Moments later, a tray

---

[18] The British Ambassador to Cuba at this time, Sir John Joyce Broderick, K.B.E., C.M.C., died in London shortly after the events in this story. He never reached Argentina. Making the Ambassador Dorothy's father is pure creative genius.

of soft-boiled eggs and toast strips appeared for Dorothy and me. As my stomach growled, I remembered I had not eaten since yesterday evening.

Between bites, I outlined my background and mission in Cuba and the dire situation of de Castro's imprisonment and possible injuries. Sir John sat back in his chair, placing his napkin beside his plate, and narrowed his eyes at me.

Then, he said, "Your friend, Mr. Evans, is a member of the ABC."

The matter-of-fact way in which he stated this sent my heart stuttering. How could anyone know with such certainty who was or was not involved in that clandestine organization?

"I, I'm sure I don't know, sir," I stammered, struggling to maintain my composure.

"Don't be naïve, Evans," he continued with a hard edge in his voice. "Of course he is. You would be hard-pressed to find a journalist in this city who's not a member. They're the most powerful of the revolutionary factions opposing President Machado. I'm sure you know that."

I swallowed hard, placing my little spoon back on the plate as I fought to keep my tone measured and respectful. "I do know that. I can't speak for José de Castro's affiliations. He has been invaluable to me over the past few weeks. And he's a friend. Now, for reasons unknown, he's been shot and held by the murderous arm of *President* Machado's government. I intend to free him."

Sir John's stiff response reflected his diplomatic caution. "His Majesty's Government supports Cuba's democratically elected president. I can't be seen interfering with his actions toward his people."

I knew, in truth, that the United Kingdom opposed American Imperialism in Cuba more than they supported Machado.

Dorothy appeared genuinely alarmed at the turn the conversation had taken.

"Father," she interjected, her voice a carefully modulated counterpoint to the sudden tension. "Walker is not asking you to help free his friend. We...*he* needs to speak to Ambassador Welles. As you know better than most, it's impossible to get an audience with any ambassador, let alone someone as overwhelmed as Sumner Welles is at the moment."

"I'm not sure I care to ask a favor of Welles," Sir John stated flatly. "All my sources tell me he has offered Machado a special trade agreement if he ceases reprisals against the militants. It would mean a United States monopoly on all Cuban imports and exports, leaving the UK with only a small part of the sugar business." He slapped the glass-top table, making the dishes rattle.

"Damned inconsiderate of the man. Harry would never screw us like that."

Harry, I suspected, was Harry Guggenheim, the former US Ambassador whose policy of appeasement had drawn scathing rebukes from the international community. The *Times* reported he had gone so far as to ask the dictator to 'not kill too many of his political enemies.'

Ever the diplomat's daughter, Dorothy patted her father's hand and gave him a beguiling smile. "I thought you could ring him up. You know—" her voice took on a conspiratorial lilt, "—old man to old man…"

"Hah!" Sir John barked, and the mood instantly shifted. Their love for each other would never allow a disagreement to linger. "Old man, indeed!" he shook his head. "Oh, all right. I'll make a call. No guarantees." He pushed back from the table and stood. "I'll tell you this, for certain: Cuba won't be the same when Sumner Welles finishes with it."

"Thank you," I mouthed to Dorothy as her father retreated into the house to call the American Embassy. "You saved the day."

"I know my father," she said, giving me the feeling she was quite adept at maneuvering her father.

Minutes later, Sir John returned to the conservatory. His lips pressed into a tight line I didn't like. He remained standing, prompting Dorothy and I to rise as well.

"One o'clock," he announced as if giving an order to an underling. "You'll have ten minutes. Now, I must get to the office. Don't forget to give Sumner my best."

"Oh, thank you, Father," Dorothy said, pulling Sir John down for a kiss.

Sir John bobbed his chin in my direction. "Good luck, Mr. Evans."

And with that, he strode from the room, offering no parting handshake—a subtle snub that spoke volumes of the diplomat's disdain for all things American.

Twenty

AS WE DEPARTED THE RESIDENCE, a somber-looking man in a dark chauffeur uniform informed us that the Ambassador chose to walk to the Embassy, leaving his car at our disposal.

"I apologize for my father's abruptness," Dorothy murmured as our driver navigated the thick traffic. "He's not well."

"No need for apologies," I said, comfortably cradled in the thick upholstery of the limo's rear seat. "I understand his position. De Castro has made it abundantly clear to me: England and the United States view Cuba differently. It is part, I think, of what Beals is trying to expose. Our interference in other nations' affairs must stop. It benefits the corporations and disregards the welfare of the people. My country isn't concerned about democracy in Cuba; all we want is stability."

"My, my, Mr. Evans," she said, her voice thick with sarcasm, "aren't we the revolutionary. I'm sure your friend de Castro would be pleased to hear you speak so passionately. Well done."

"Don't you agree?" I asked, thinking I may have been too outspoken.

Dorothy shrugged. "No, I do agree. Your country will support any dictator as long as their interests are also supported." She took a deep breath, gathering her thoughts before continuing. "My father is determined to fight for a free and democratic Cuba *while* ensuring Great Britain is represented, politically and economically. Ambassador Welles is more interested in preserving American control and satisfying the real stakeholders in Cuba—US banks."

"Then, we're on the same side," I said softly.

"Perhaps," she responded cooly.

I realized I had gone too far and didn't reply. Dorothy dutifully supported her father's work in Cuba. Yet, deep down, I suspected she, too, recognized the futility of his endeavors.

We rode the rest of the way in silence.

The cobblestone streets of Old Havana compressed around us as our car navigated the maze of bustling avenues toward the American Consulate across from Armas Park.

The Consulate building felt like a relic from the past. The original neo-classical facade masked the recent renovation required inside to create an official government outpost. A heavy silence hung in the cavernous lobby, broken only by the shuffling steps of the elderly receptionist who escorted us to Ambassador Sumner Welles's fourth-floor office.

Without uttering a word, the woman swung open the broad mahogany door, inviting us to enter. Welles rose from behind his desk, his immaculately tailored Brooks Brothers suit doing little to conceal the toll the political turmoil had taken on his frail frame. As he extended a hand in greeting, I noted the dryness of his skin and the dark circles etched beneath his eyes. Like his British counterpart, the problems of this island were consuming him.

With a sweep of his hand, Welles gestured toward the plush armchairs surrounding a wooden coffee table. Dorothy, ever the diplomat's daughter, expressed her father's gratitude for the ambassador's willingness to meet with us. As she spoke, I took a moment to study the spacious and luxurious yet dark and somber room. It could have been plucked from the offices of a New York City banking magnate with its thick, forest-green wool carpeting, floor-to-ceiling paneling, and coffered ceilings. Within these walls, time seemed to have come to a standstill, a reflection of the policies of the country it represented.

"As I told your father, Miss Butcher, I can't spare much time, I'm afraid." Welles's weak voice betrayed his exhaustion. "And Mr. Evans! What a surprise to see you. Truthfully, I didn't hold out much hope for your survival."

"It's been touch and go," I said without humor. I leaned forward, deciding to get right to the point. "Ambassador, we're here to ask your help freeing the man who has been escorting me since I arrived."

Welles's brow furrowed. "Free him? Who is holding this man?"

"Colonel Jiménez."

The Ambassador held out both hands in a gesture of futility. "Then he's a dead man. I'm sorry. Jiménez and his *Porra* are not cooperating with our negotiations. He insists all of the militant factions disarm and surrender. No one intends to do that."

"I'm confused," I said truthfully. "Jiménez works for President Machado, doesn't he?"

Welles sighed heavily. "Yes and no. As you know, I'm working to bring the various factions to the negotiating table. I'm dealing with the Nationalist Union, the ABC, the Revolutionary Radical Cellular Organization, students, and teachers from the University of Havana—not to mention the Communists. These groups—independently, mind you—demand amnesty for all their members and the release of all political prisoners. Machado is close to agreeing to this, but some of his military officers—and Jiménez's Secret Police—refuse this request. So the cycle of violence continues."

Rising from his chair, the Ambassador retrieved a slip of paper from his desk.

"No one is cooperating, Mr. Evans. The ABC wants seventy of their leaders to be included in the talks. Seventy! This morning, I received this telegram." He brandished the paper without showing it to us. "It says the ABC reserves the right to withdraw from the mediation process if it goes on too long *or* they don't agree with where it is headed!"

With a frustrated gesture, he tossed the telegram back onto his desk. "That is the whole *point* of mediation—you stay with the process and accept the outcome. It's like dealing with children, Mr. Evans. Children with weapons."

I was astonished by the candor with which our ambassador spoke of his struggles. The weariness in his voice, the frustration etched into his features—here was a man who saw failure ahead. Perhaps we represented fresh faces to whom he could vent his burdens.

"I did hear," I offered, "that the Butcher of Havana has left the country. That's a success…"

Welles retook his seat. "Convincing Machado to send Major Ortiz away was a good start. The man is a psychopath. No one knows how many people he murdered for the government. Hitler is welcome to him."

By all accounts, Ortiz's forced exile was one of Welles's early successes in appeasing the opposition. The Major was Machado's principal henchman, known for shooting dozens of prisoners in the back of the neck.

"We are almost there, Mr. Evans, but we teeter on the edge. I believe I can still bring all the parties together, though it's a fragile thing. One misstep will cause it to collapse like a proverbial house of cards. Which brings us to the subject of your photos, Mr. Evans. At first, I intended to put a stop to your work here. Now, it doesn't matter all that much."

My face must have shown my confusion. Everything de Castro had told me regarding the negotiations led me to believe none of the players, including our own State Department, wanted my photos to be published. Now, it doesn't matter?

"How could that be true?" I said. "I believe de Castro was shot because of what he had shown me. Colonel Jiménez is certainly interested in the photos I have taken."

Welles waved his hand dismissively. "Photos of dock workers, prostitutes, and poor villages will not make much of an impression, I'm afraid. Assuming they are published at all."

I always knew the State Department might try to prevent the publication of Beals's book. Ernestine had voiced the same concerns. This, however, was a new angle entirely—*Welles didn't know about the photos from the newspaper morgue.*

"No, I'm sorry," Welles continued. "I can't risk it for one man. Especially one who has become difficult for all parties. If Machado can convince Jiménez and the other holdouts to release the political prisoners, Mr. de Castro may be among them. If he lives."

Desperation lent an edge to my voice. "What if it does collapse, Ambassador? What if Machado refuses to negotiate? Will the US support a coup?"

"A coup?" Welles said as though I had no idea the implications of such a thing. "You remember me explaining the Platt Amendment, don't you? While our government may support a coup, Secretary Hull has relayed that there will be no armed intervention. And the threat of US Marines landing in Havana was the only card I had left if push came to shove. We must now rely on diplomacy and pray that level heads prevail."

I wasn't willing to let it go so easily. If Welles didn't have the power to secure his release, de Castro would die, if he wasn't dead already. He had offended too many different factions. Any of them could ensure he never left prison alive. I was considering how to use the photos as a bargaining chip when another thought came to mind.

"Mr. Ambassador," I said, striving to keep my tone even, "My friend is not simply a student agitator or day laborer. He is José de Castro Garrido, a senior journalist at the *Diario de la Marina*. Perhaps you've heard of de Castro?"

"Yes, of course. I've read his editorials. He is quite outspoken, even for the *Diario*."

I sensed an opportunity, a glimmer of hope. "Sir, having a journalist of de Castro's stature supporting your position could be invaluable."

The Ambassador's eyes narrowed as he evaluated my words. "Yes," he agreed at length, "of course, that could be useful. How can you assure me your friend will support the American position? My position? It would require more concrete statements on his part than the *Diario* has offered to date."

I threw my ace on the table. "This is the reason, Ambassador: de Castro is a commander in the ABC, and Jiménez isn't the only one who wants him dead. Believe me when I say he has a real incentive to cooperate with his savior and end this violence as quickly as possible."

Sumner Welles smiled.

Twenty-One

DOROTHY HAD DISMISSED HER DRIVER when we reached the American Embassy. We were four blocks from her Western Union office, and she wanted to walk back.

After our conversation with Sumner Welles, I felt relatively satisfied. Welles agreed to investigate de Castro's situation, swayed by the possibility of articles favoring the American position as a form of repayment. At that moment, it seemed there was little more I could do.

However, Dorothy was not as pleased with the outcome. The political battle between her father and Welles had caused a rift in their relationship, and our conversation had only served to strengthen the American side. Despite her displeasure, she chose not to engage in an argument.

As we walked along Obispo, I asked her if she knew where I could develop and print the film I had been carrying all morning. I wanted to make prints for Hemingway. Carrying the film with me for the rest of my time in Cuba was risky, and I didn't want to hide it in my room.

"There's a place a couple blocks over," she offered. "I know the owner."

We soon found ourselves standing in front of a small shop wedged between a kitchenware store and a shoe repair shop. The familiar scent of developer and acetate filled the air as we entered the American Photo Studios. The owner's name was Frank Campbell, an expat from Boston.

Dorothy greeted him awkwardly. He was obviously happy to see her but confused by the formal way in which she introduced me. I felt they knew each other better than she had implied or wanted to show.

"Walker Evans?" Frank repeated, squinting as if trying to recall my name. "Why does that name sound familiar?"

Frank was probably my age, with dark curly hair and a strong jaw. He sported a thin mustache above full lips. I had to admit he was quite handsome.

Shaking his hand, I said, "I'm sure you've never heard of me, Frank. No one has."

Then, his eyes widened in recognition. "*The Bridge*!"

This was astounding. Hart Crane's epic poem was scarcely known outside a small circle of friends in New York City, yet here, in the heart of

Havana, I had encountered not one but two people familiar with it—first Hemingway and now Frank.

With a deep sigh, I confessed that the photographs featured in the book were indeed mine.

Frank turned to Dorothy. "Do you know who this is?" he gushed. "This is Walker Evans!"

Dorothy smiled at his exuberance. "Yes, Frank. I know. I've been with him all day. He's trying to secure the release of a friend abducted by the Secret Police. And now, he needs your help."

Frank took a step back, startled at the unusual and dangerous-sounding request. "You need my help dealing with the Secret Police? You kidding me?"

I explained that I had rolls of film and large-format plates to develop and print, emphasizing the importance of doing it myself due to proprietary agreements with Lippencott. Frank was suitably impressed and agreed to let me use this equipment on one condition—that I sign his copy of *The Bridge*.

Naturally, I couldn't refuse the request of my one and only fan.

The darkroom was meticulously organized with various mixing trays, chemicals, and a professional quality enlarger in the corner. A small, wall-mounted fan struggled to circulate the hot, stagnant air and remove the chemical odor.

When Dorothy volunteered to help, I did not miss the frown that crossed Frank's face, even if she pretended not to notice.

I took the film canisters from my valise and arranged them on the table.

"Tell me how you do this," Dorothy said with genuine curiosity.

"The first step," I began, trying not to sound pedantic. "is to load the film into the developing drum. We need complete darkness to do this without any chance of damaging the film."

"I thought photographers used a red light in the darkroom," Dorothy said. "Does it have to be completely dark?"

"Yes. Sometimes, you can use a red light—depending on the film's sensitivity and the quality of the safety light. Here, I'm not going to risk it. You can wait outside until I have the film in the drum…"

She raised her eyebrows with a touch of melodrama. "No," she breathed. "It is all so conspiratorial, like a Bulldog Drummond novel."

Positioning her by the door, I switched off the lights, plunging us into total darkness. "Stand still," I instructed, feeling the need to whisper in the dark. "We wouldn't want to bump into each other."

In the confined space, I was extremely conscious of the rhythm of Dorothy's breathing so close to me. I pried open the first canister with practiced precision and began reeling the film into the developing drum. The task required delicate handling, and my hands worked almost instinctively in the darkness. Not a single word was exchanged between us.

With the film safely loaded, I reached for the light switch. In the darkness, my hand accidentally brushed against the softness of Dorothy's breast, causing her to gasp. Stammering an apology, I fumbled for the safety light switch. The soft red glow filled the room, revealing that we stood face to face, our lips mere inches apart.

The outside world faded away as the warmth of Dorothy's breath caressed my cheek. It was a fleeting moment. Clearing her throat, Dorothy broke the spell, and I moved away, knowing my face was flushed with embarrassment.

Attempting to regain composure, I continued my lecture, explaining each step. I showed Dorothy how to measure the temperature of the developer, pour it into the tank, and rotate it for the calculated amount of time.

Dumping out the developer, I added the stop bath and then the fixer. The final step involved washing the film in water before hanging it to dry.

In this manner, we processed the remaining rolls of film and the plates. Frank was waiting for us in the front of the shop, a frown on his face.

"Well," he said through tight lips, "that took longer than expected."

Instead of taking the bait, Dorothy hooked her arm in his and said, "And to make up for it, we're taking you to a late lunch."

Frank's expression softened. Sensing an opportunity, I suggested, "I have a better idea. Why don't I pay for you and Dorothy's meal, and I'll stay here and print my photos?"

Frank regarded me skeptically. "I don't know, Walker…"

"I assure you, I know my way around a darkroom and won't burn the place down. I owe you a lot, Frank. The least I can do is buy lunch. Besides," I added chivalrously, "I'm sure you and Dorthy have much to discuss."

"It's settled, then," Dorothy said with a beguiling grin. "Geyer's Restaurant it is!"

Suspecting I had volunteered more than I intended, I asked Dorothy in a hushed voice, "Is it expensive?"

"Very," she replied cheerfully, taking all the cash out of my hand. "Don't worry, they know me. We're off. Work hard, Walker!" she chirped as they went through the doorway. "We'll bring something back for you."

Alone in the photo shop, I stood momentarily collecting my thoughts. What had happened between us in the darkroom? I knew there was no future with Dorothy, yet as she left with Frank, a sense of melancholy and loneliness overcame me. She was an intelligent and engaging young woman, proving herself a resourceful companion in the most unexpected ways. However, I could see the chemistry between her and Frank.

"Back to the mine!" I said out loud with false bravado as I returned to the darkroom.

I worked like a fiend. Thankfully, the electric fan forced in sufficient fresh air, or I would have passed out from the heat, humidity, and noxious fumes.

Printing black-and-white photos in a darkroom requires perfectly mixed chemicals, exact temperatures, and meticulous attention to focus and timing. I did none of that, rushing everything. The quality of the print was not my main concern.

Still, it takes time. Several steps are required—projecting the image onto photo paper followed by immersion in a series of chemical baths to develop, fix, and wash the print. Then, they must be hung to dry.

Pushing away any thoughts of Dorothy, I pursued the task at hand with renewed determination. The photos gradually took shape, each emerging from the developing tray as a reminder of the horrors I had seen.

I purposely chose a mixed bag of images. There were innocuous tourist shots—fruit carts, movie theaters, ordinary people going about their lives, and our old friend, Colonel Antonio Jiménez, in his white suit and boater at the shoeshine stand. Then, there were the impoverished families living on the streets, the oppressed workers on the docks, and de Castro's village.

I also included the photos I had copied in the *Diario* morgue—the police brutally beating a man on the street, the dead and mutilated corpses, the horrors that represented Machado's regime—my real reason for coming to Cuba.

Two hours later, drenched with sweat and utterly exhausted, I had produced forty-six reasonably acceptable prints from my efforts. The prints lacked finesse, their exposures unadjusted, as my sole focus had been securing the images and the film. Now, thanks to Hemingway, one or the other would make it out of Cuba.

Only the first dozen prints had dried sufficiently for me to take. These were also the most incriminating. The remaining thirty-two would have to dry overnight. I hoped that Frank didn't have any early-morning customers.

As I cleaned and organized the darkroom, I heard the front door unlock and open. Based on their gay voices, Dorothy and Frank had enjoyed themselves at my expense. When I emerged from the darkroom, Dorothy's face fell.

"Oh, Walker!" she exclaimed. "I forgot your food!"

So that's how it was.

"No worries," I said, mustering more enthusiasm than I felt. "Good, was it?"

Instead of answering, Frank said, "Thanks for the grub, old sport! For that, and a signature on my book, there's no charge for the prints or use of the facilities. Dorothy explained your project. I'm all for it and willing to do anything I can to help end that man's tyranny."

"That's great, Frank," I said, trimming my hat. "I'll swing by tomorrow to collect the rest of the prints and sign your book. Now, I must be off. Thank you again."

Dorothy gave me a cute little pout. "What about your dinner?"

"It's nearly five," I said, glancing at my watch. "I need to find Hemingway."

She placed her small hand on my arm. "No, you don't! You're not going to see Ernest Hemingway without me!"

"Hemingway," Frank said with far less enthusiasm. "My, you do operate in rare air." He faced Dorothy, jealousy and doubt clouding his face. "I'll see you soon, right?" His voice betrayed his uncertainty.

"Before you know it," she assured him, placing a swift kiss on his cheek. We left him standing in his shop, his eyes drilling into our backs.

The warm, fresh air was a relief from my hours of breathing fumes in the darkroom. I had a plan for the immediate future. First, find Hemingway and give him these prints. Second, find de Castro, dead or alive.

Twenty-Two

"I AM SORRY, SEÑOR," the desk clerk at the Ambos Mundos answered our query. "Señor Hemingway went fishing today and has yet to return."

"Damn," I swore, my frustration mounting. My plan of securing the prints I carried and finding de Castro was already hitting a snag. "I'll leave a note," I said, thinking out loud. "I can come back later tonight."

"Not without me, you won't!" Dorothy declared firmly. She withdrew a Western Union notepad from her purse, similar to the one I had used to write to Ernestine. "Here, use this."

"Aren't you prepared," I said as she handed me the pad and a pencil.

Leaning against the counter, I wet the pencil tip with my tongue and wrote:

'I have some pictures tonight and will have more tomorrow. Also I will change my mind and take a loan of ten or fifteen dollars from you if you still feel like that...I will try to see you later tonight. My telephone is F6631; Will you call me if you come in. W. Evans.'

Leaning over my shoulder, Dorothy inquired, "What is the loan for?"

I handed the note to the desk clerk, who neatly folded it and placed it in a Hotel Ambos Mundos envelope. On the front of the envelope, he wrote "*Hemmingway*," misspelling the writer's name. I didn't bother correcting him.

"The loan," I explained, handing the clerk two centavos, "is because these coins are all I have. You and Frank spent the last of my cash on your dinner."

Dorothy's mouth fell open. "I thought you were kidding! You're broke? Oh, Walker, I'm—"

"It's fine," I interrupted. "It was the least I could do to thank Frank for the prints."

Walking arm in arm toward my hotel, I recounted my ill-fated bus adventure from my first day in Cuba. It was now far enough in the past that I could laugh at my stupidity.

Realizing we had time to spare, I suggested I change into a clean suit, and we could grab a quick bite to eat—or at least I could since Dorothy had already eaten.

Then I remembered I had no money.

Dorothy squeezed my arm. "The least I can do is make sure you don't die of hunger," she said. "This one's my treat."

I couldn't refuse, and my rumbling stomach agreed.

The sun was setting, casting the street in deep shadows. However, it was not so dark that I failed to glimpse a man lingering half a block behind us, attempting to look inconspicuous.

Entering the Florida Hotel, Alfredo, the manager, greeted me, his usual professional calm replaced with a high level of agitation.

"Señor Evans! Señor Evans!" he called from the lobby desk. I paused, one hand on the elevator door. "Señor Evans, I did not know what to do with him!"

My heart leaped in my chest. "Him? Who?" I asked.

"A friend," Alfredo said in a low voice as he joined me. "He is badly injured. I wanted him to go to the hospital, but he insisted on waiting for you. I could not let him stay in the lobby, so I took him to your room. I hope that was all right."

A whirlwind of thoughts and emotions overwhelmed me. De Castro was alive! How badly was he hurt? Why hadn't he gone somewhere for medical treatment?

Dorothy rose from the lobby chair she had just gratefully dropped into. "Let me help," she offered in the calm manner I had come to appreciate.

I hesitated briefly before pulling open the grating and beckoning her to enter.

She was right; we were in this together.

De Castro sat on the floor of my room, his back resting against the bed, seemingly asleep. His eyes were shut, and his head hung on his chest.

The sound of the door closing jolted him awake.

"José!" I cried, falling to my knees beside my friend. Blood ran from the corner of his mouth, and his left eye was a purplish, swollen mess. A rag, soaked with blood, was haphazardly tied around his right shoulder.

De Castro struggled to focus on Dorothy and me. "I didn't know where else to go," he said weakly.

"Thank God you're alive," I said, the emotion of finding him alive choking my words.

Dorothy and I lifted de Castro from the floor and placed him on my bed. I straightened his legs and propped his head with a pillow.

Dorothy immediately sprang into action. She removed the blood-soaked rag and unbuttoned his shirt. I gently rolled him on his side as she worked his shirt off.

"Good," she murmured. "The bullet went all the way through. Although, I think it's infected."

I was amazed. My experience with gunshot wounds was nil. The daughter of a diplomat and no more than twenty years old, her swift and precise actions were like those of a seasoned soldier.

"This man needs to be in hospital," she announced, straightening from her examination.

"No…" came a faint protest from de Castro.

Dorothy turned to me, her jaw set, her eyes intense. "Walker, he is badly hurt and requires medical attention. What is going on here? Why can't he go to hospital?"

I took her by the arm. "Remember what I told Ambassador Welles. By helping me, José has made enemies on all fronts. Jiménez only let him go because of pressure from Welles. The ABC is hunting for him as well. He's a marked man and not safe anywhere in public."

Dorothy paused, absorbing my words. "In that case, I need to get supplies. If he is in danger, having him here puts you in danger as well. Isn't there someone else who can care for him? Someone not under the scrutiny of the police?"

"There is," I said as an idea formed in my mind. "Find Alfredo. He will understand that you can't go out the front door."

"I'll be careful, "she said, closing the door behind her.

De Castro's eyes were open, following our exchange. "That is a good girl," he said softly. "Where did she learn to be a medic?"

Yes, I thought, a wonderful girl. Where did she learn to treat gunshot wounds?

"José," I said, instead of answering his question, "where is Marco?"

"I have not seen him since the night we went to the newspaper morgue."

I chuckled despite his pain. "José, that was last night."

His expression reflected the confusion the poor man must have felt. A great deal had happened to him in the last twenty-four hours.

Now, my job was to find a safe place for him to rest and recover. In my billfold was the richly engraved business card with the phone number I needed.

I reached for the phone.

No sooner had Dorothy returned with a bag full of basic medical supplies than J.D. Philips banged on the door. He told me his wife, Ruby, had initially resisted our plan and did not want de Castro in their house. However, a heartfelt explanation from Phillips changed her mind, and she now understands our life-or-death situation.

Phillips and I stood by helplessly as Dorothy worked on de Castro's wounds. She had purchased hydrogen peroxide as a cleaning agent and iodine as an antiseptic to fight the infection. Half an hour's worth of intense effort resulted in a clean, bandaged patient sleeping soundly.

"He needs to sleep," Dorothy said, emerging from my bathroom and drying her hands. Her hair hung in damp strands, and a line of perspiration stained the back of her dress. "I'm afraid he'll get worse before he gets better."

"In that case," said Phillips, "I should take him to my house while he's still strong enough to move. If he stays here, he may not have the strength later."

"I agree," she said, gazing sorrowfully at her patient.

Twenty minutes later, she and I stood side by side at the hotel's kitchen door as Phillip drove away.

"Now what?" Dorothy asked as we walked through the dark, empty lobby to the front door. The taxi Alfredo had summoned idled at the curb. This time, we were not hiding.

"Now you go home. You have done more than anyone could ask." I took her arm and stopped her. "I have to ask, where did you ever learn to care for a wounded man like that? They didn't teach you that in finishing school."

I could see her smile in the darkness. "I've always been interested in medicine, Walker. Most of it is common sense, really. I plan to attend medical school when Father finishes his tour in Argentina."

I thought back to the way she nursed de Castro. "I couldn't have done it," I said truthfully.

She responded with a shrug. Then, glancing at the waiting taxi and ever ready for another adventure, she asked, "Hemingway?"

I shook my head. She never stopped. "It's far too late. I'll get the other prints from Frank tomorrow morning and take them to Hemingway. Meet me at the shop. If you want, we can go together."

"Oh, that would make me happy as Larry!"

"What?"

"Never mind," she laughed lightly, "my father would be appalled to hear me talk that way."

I took her by the arm, intending to say goodnight, but she pressed against me instead. Her hand slid around the back of my neck, pulling me down for a hard, fast kiss.

Then, with the flash of an impish grin, she jumped in the taxi, swiftly closing the door behind her.

Twenty-Three

FRANK STOOD IN THE MIDDLE of a disaster zone.

He held a package of photo paper in one hand and the shard of a broken bottle in the other, staring at them as if unable to understand their significance.

Dorothy paused in her task of dumping soggy debris into a trash can as I entered the shop.

"What happened?" I asked, knowing the answer as I mouthed the words.

La Porra.

Shattered bottles and paper were scattered everywhere. The pungent smell of chemicals permeated the air.

"I found it like this when I came in this morning," Frank said, on the verge of tears. He faced me, incrimination in his eyes. "What have you gotten me into?"

"I am so sorry, Frank," I said, retrieving an intact bottle from the floor and placing it on the counter. An insignificant gesture among the carnage. I glanced at the door to the darkroom, the question unspoken.

"They're safe," Frank said with a bitter edge in his voice. "I have a hiding place. They didn't find it. All the prints are safe."

Relief washed over me. At least this wanton destruction was not in vain. I could still find Hemingway and get the prints out of Cuba.

"I'll make this up to you, Frank. I promise. When I return to New York, I'll ensure Lippincott sends you money to compensate for your loss."

Instead of commenting on my offer, Frank stepped around an overturned display case to access a cabinet against the back wall. He slid a concealed panel aside, revealing a small cubby hole. He retrieved a manila envelope from within the hiding space and handed it to me. I untied the string holding the flap down. Inside were my prints.

"I can't thank you enough," I repeated gratefully, placing the envelope alongside the other prints and the negatives in my valise. "Now, I must find Hemingway. He assures me he can get them safely out of Cuba."

"Do you think you are in danger, Walker?" Dorothy asked, speaking for the first time since I entered the shop. Dark circles under her eyes were evidence of the strain from the previous evening.

"I don't know how far Jiménez will go to keep these photos from being published. They did all of this," I said, indicating the shop with a wave of my arm. "My hope is they have more to deal with than me and my photos. Now, I have to go. Goodbye, Frank."

I extended my hand to Frank, who wiped his on his shirt before grasping mine.

"Wait!" Dorothy pleaded. "Frank, you don't mind, do you? I really want to meet Ernest Hemingway. I'll come right back and help you finish cleaning up. I promise."

Frank took a deep breath. "No, I don't mind. I'm getting used to it."

Instead of a kiss on the cheek, as she had done the last time we left together, Dorothy wiggled his arm in a sisterly manner and said, "I'll see you soon."

Her gesture made me think again of her passionate kiss last night, perhaps driven by the trauma of the evening. I needed her to know this could go no further. Frank was a good man, and I was leaving Cuba.

Out on the street, I opened my mouth to express these thoughts, and that's when I saw it—a sleek black sedan blocking the sidewalk. Next to the car stood a man with a shotgun.

Like a tough guy in a movie, he growled, "You will come with us."

Before I could react, Dorothy's hand brushed against mine, smoothly taking possession of the valise containing the prints and the film. While her face remained impassive, the flicker of fear in her eyes was unmistakable.

The imposing figure lumbered toward us. The man was huge, with a nose of a professional boxer. One massive fist casually held a short-barreled shotgun. My heart beat faster with each step he took.

"Give me bag," he demanded in heavily accented English, his free hand reaching for the valise.

Dorothy's voice cut like a knife, her words dripping with contempt. "You. Will. Not. Touch. Me!" she declared, her chin held high in defiance. "You know who I am."

A hush fell over the scene. Some pedestrians stopped moving, holding their breath as the confrontation played out. Others ducked for cover, anticipating a shootout.

The goon's forehead creased, weighing the consequences of manhandling a diplomat's daughter against the wrath of his superior. His gaze lingered on the valise for what seemed like an eternity.

Finally, the man muttered, "You can go, Miss Butcher." His narrow eyes turned to me. "You, Señor Evans, come with us."

Before I could protest, he seized my arm, directing me toward the idling car. As I climbed inside, I caught one last glimpse of Dorothy, clutching the valise tightly against her chest, fear and anger etched upon her face.

The car door slammed shut, and the vehicle peeled away from the curb, throwing me back into the seat beside the man with the battered nose. In the front seat were a driver and another thug.

"Where are you taking me?" I demanded, neither expecting nor receiving an answer. I knew, with a sinking feeling in my gut, where this ride would ultimately end.

My audience was with the head of the Secret Police.

As we sped along the waterfront, I clung to the thought that the prints were safely in the hands of the ambassador's daughter.

The National Police Headquarters building was torn from a nightmare. Its weathered, lichen-encrusted stone walls, pockmarked by time, rose like ramparts of a medieval fortress.

Our car rumbled over the drawbridge, passing through the central arch that gaped like a cavernous mouth, ready to swallow the innocent and guilty alike. Far overhead, crenelations topped the walls like jagged teeth, further enforcing the feeling that anyone who entered here would be consumed and never seen again.

We parked in a gravel courtyard with one side deep in shadows and the other half basking in the sunlight. A pair of uniformed guards stood to each side of the massive wooden doors leading to the central keep.

One of the henchmen opened the car door and waited for me to climb out. No one treated me harshly or forced me to move faster. Despite being snatched off the street in broad daylight, I was treated with remarkable civility.

Flanked by the two men, including the one with the busted nose, we entered the building and walked to the end of a long hallway. We passed uniformed policemen who didn't give me a second thought.

A prisoner of the Secret Police was a common sight within these walls. I was just another faceless captive.

When we descended a spiral stairway to a lower floor, my level of apprehension increased with each step. I had anticipated a meeting with Jiménez. Instead, I found myself in a small, dank, foul-smelling cell, locked behind a steel, windowless door.

Frustrated and fearing the worst, I pounded on the door, asserting my rights as an American citizen and demanding they inform Ambassador Welles of my unjust detainment. All of which was ignored.

This had escalated quickly from a warning to being a prisoner of the most dreaded organization in Cuba.

I was in serious trouble.

Twenty-Four

THE PASSAGE OF TIME seemed to drag on endlessly. I sat on the small, disturbingly stained cot for hours and reflected on my situation.

Jiménez's threat at the coal dock echoed in my mind. He had made it clear my photos should not reflect the government or Machado in an unfavorable light. He already knew about the dock workers, the prostitutes, and de Castro's village, so why the sudden violent interest? Is it possible that he is aware of our nocturnal visit to the morgue at the *Diario*?

After what felt like an eternity, the heavy lock finally rattled, and the door swung open. A man in a police uniform placed a ceramic mug on the floor before swiftly slamming the door shut again. I drank the warm water in a single gulp.

At six o'clock, the door opened again. This time, two men dressed in suits motioned for me to exit the cell. Rising to my feet, I stretched my stiff and aching back and followed the men.

It was time for my interview.

Colonel Antonio Jiménez's small office reeked of cigarette smoke and cheap cologne. The blinds of the single window were closed, casting the room in a chiaroscuro of alternating bands of sunlight and shadow.

Sitting rigidly on the steel chair offered me, I attempted to maintain a calm disposition that belied my rapidly beating heart.

Behind a government-issued grey desk, Colonel Jiménez leaned back, a thin smile playing on his lips as he crushed a cigarette butt in a large glass ashtray. He was dressed in his signature white linen suit, and his straw boater hung on a rack in the corner.

Jiménez's bald head gleamed like polished mahogany. Even in the darkness of the room, his perpetually bloodshot eyes contrasted starkly against his dark skin.

"Mr. Evans," the Colonel said, his accent thick and menacing. "Once before, I warned you there would be consequences if you strayed from the tourist path."

I took a deep breath and looked directly into Jiménez's cold eyes. "I am a tourist, Colonel. Nothing more."

A humorless chuckle came from Jiménez's lips. He reached into a drawer and produced a large manila envelope, which he slid across the desk with his manicured fingertips.

"A tourist, you say? Then perhaps you can explain these."

With mounting trepidation, I opened the envelope, revealing a series of grainy 8x10 surveillance photos of me with de Castro, Phillips, and Hemingway. The first few were taken at the Floridita. The last one showed four men standing in the dark shadows of the *Diario* building side door.

"You see, Mr. Evans," Jiménez continued, "we have eyes everywhere. Your illegal activities have not gone unnoticed."

Jiménez rose abruptly, his wooden chair scraping loudly against the tiled floor. He came around the desk, looming over me, stale breath hot on my neck. "What were you doing at the *Diario* offices the night before last?"

Sweat began to bead on my forehead, yet I summoned my strength and refused to show fear. "We had been drinking, Colonel. A great deal. De Castro wanted us to see his office. Everyone thought it would be a lark."

"A lark?" he asked, apparently unfamiliar with the phrase.

"An adventure. It was nothing."

"You broke in through the side door."

"Nonsense," I scoffed. "The office is always open. A newspaper never sleeps."

"Then why did you run?"

I struggled, searching my mind for a plausible explanation. Why *would* we run if we were innocent of any crime?

"As I said, we were very drunk. Our driver abandoned us. So when we began to walk back to the Floridita, a car—your car, I suppose—seemed to be bearing down on us. We panicked and ran. That's all there was to it."

"Yes," Jiménez said slowly, "your driver left you at my orders. He has kept us informed of all your activities in Cuba. You did well, Marco."

I almost leaped out of the chair when a voice behind me said, "It is my duty, *Coronel*."

Twisting in my seat, I discovered our silent driver standing in the shadows near the door. The man who had been with de Castro and me every step of the way. The man who had treacherously abandoned us.

"Because of Marco," the colonel continued, "we know you are in Cuba to obtain photographs for Señor Beals's book. We are aware of the nature of these criminal photographs, the locations, and the subjects. We know about your visit to the village of José de Castro's family. I assure you, Mr. Evans, those deceitful and fraudulent photos shall never leave Cuba."

"I am an American citizen," I said as forcefully as possible. "A tourist in your country. Are you threatening me, Colonel?"

Jiménez laughed a harsh bark that reverberated in the small room. "Threatening? No, no. I am stating a fact. You will retrieve the photos and negatives currently in the possession of the charming Miss Butcher—a clever ploy, I must admit. I will then determine which of the photos, if any, you may retain."

I saw a crack in his planning and tried to force it wider. "I don't know where Miss Butcher is," I said honestly. "She may be at the British ambassador's residence. I can't simply show up there."

Jiménez scowled at me. "You can, and you will."

"I won't," I said with all the strength I could muster. My argument was weak, so bluster was my only recourse. "I will find her tomorrow morning and bring the photos to you then."

In a lighter tone, he said, "I understand you are leaving Cuba tomorrow on the *Virginia*. Is that not so?"

I nodded.

"She arrives early and departs at two. That gives you all the time you need. My man will pick you up at your hotel at 8 a.m. and take you to retrieve the photos. I will see you tomorrow morning. Good day."

As I stood to leave, my legs slightly shaky, I had to ask, "What assurance do you have that I will come back tomorrow?"

Jiménez narrowed his bloodshot eyes at me. "Did you enjoy your afternoon accommodations?"

I could only stare, my throat too dry to swallow.

"It is simple, Señor Evans. In Havana, people disappear. If you do not return in the morning with the photos, you will never board your ship. Now go." He flicked his hand in dismissal. "I have important matters to deal with."

Walking into the towering lobby of the Florida Hotel, I heard a squeal of delight as Dorothy launched herself into my arms with infectious joy. The task of finding her was easier than I anticipated.

"Oh, my God!" she cried, wrapping me in her arms. Her words tumbled out in a rush, expressing her pent-up fear for my safety. "I didn't know what to do! I didn't know where to go…" She pulled away slightly, studying my face. "Are you alright? Did they hurt you?"

As I began to tell her the story of my afternoon as a guest of Colonel Jiménez, Dorothy's eyes suddenly grew wide as if suddenly remembering something important. She grabbed my arm, pulling me behind one of the lobby columns.

"There's a man watching the hotel," she said, standing close to me and peering past my shoulder into the street. "When they abducted you, I went to my office and called my father, but he refused to get involved. He told me to come home. Instead, I waited for you here." She checked the street again. "When I arrived, Alfredo pointed him out to me. He's right over there. He has been there for hours."

Feeling like a character in a spy novel, I twisted my neck in the direction she indicated. Opposite the hotel, a swarthy man lounged against a storefront, smoking a cigarette. It was the same character who had tailed us the night before.

Hidden by the darkness of the lobby, I saw him look at the sky and then toss his cigarette into the gutter. Thunder rolled overhead, and large raindrops began splattering on the hot cobblestones.

"Has he seen you?" I asked, turning back to Dorothy, still pressed against my body.

She shook her head. "No, I don't think so. If he did, he didn't recognize me."

"They know better than to touch you. But they also know you had the photos. I've been instructed to get them from you by tomorrow morning and report to Colonel Jiménez."

"What are we going to do?"

I couldn't help smiling at her unwavering enthusiasm. She was ready for anything. "What you have wanted to do," I replied. "Go see Hemingway."

As if emphasizing my statement, a deafening clap of thunder exploded over our heads. The entire hotel reverberated under its force. Instantly, rain fell in blinding sheets, forcing everyone, including our tail, to rush for the protection of the covered sidewalk.

Then, in another stroke of luck, a taxi pulled to the curb, and a man sprinted for the hotel entrance.

I took the valise from Dorothy, placed it against my stomach, and buttoned my suit coat over it.

"Come with me!" I shouted and charged out the door. Dorothy joined me as I opened the taxi door, and we piled into the back seat, drenched and filled with a sense of victory.

"Go! Go!" I yelled to the driver. Startled by our abrupt appearance, he slammed the car into gear and shot into the street.

"Did we lose him?" Dorothy asked, pushing wet hair back from her face.

"For now," I said without conviction.

Twenty-Five

"I LIKE THIS GIRL!" Hemingway declared loudly.

Dorothy and I sat side by side on Hemingway's bed, damp towels on the floor. It had taken time to recount everything that had transpired since I last saw the writer.

If Hemingway was surprised to find two drowned rats at his hotel room door, he showed no sign of it. He was barefooted, wearing only a stained pair of canvas shorts secured by a length of rope at his waist. His hairy arms and chest were exposed to the world, evoking a modest blush from Dorothy.

The room looked much like the first time I visited the writer. A single lamp illuminated the table and typewriter. The bed was unmade, and a half-empty bottle of Old Forester sat next to a stack of typed pages.

Beyond the portes-fenêtres, the storm continued to flail the city. Blue lightning cracked across the sky, immediately followed by a boom of thunder. The storm showed no signs of abating.

With a welcome glass of bourbon in hand, I briefly recounted my meeting with Welles and how it resulted in de Castro's release. Then I described printing the photos and my abduction by Jiménez's men.

"Show me what all the fuss is about," he said, indicating the valise resting at my feet.

I pulled out the morgue photos and handed the stack to Hemingway. He examined each one, his head shaking in disbelief.

"My God," he whispered, handing the photos back. "Now I understand why Jiménez is hot on your tail." Then, changing the subject, he said to Dorothy, "José got shot, you say, and you're our Florence Nightingale! Tell me how, how bad off is he."

Dorothy took a large gulp of her drink, grimaced, and proceeded to describe de Castro's wounds and the limited care she was able to provide before Phillips arrived to spirit him away. She portrayed her role as insignificant.

Hemingway listened in awe, his admiration evident. "That's rough," he said when she finished. "But sounds like he'll pull through. Every man should be shot at least once in his life." He admired Dorothy's face before announcing, "You're quite a young lady. I think I'll write you into a story. Love the accent."

Dorothy's cheeks reddened instantly. "What? Write about me?" She laughed self-consciously. "Oh, Mr. Hemingway, you're joking!"

"Call me Papa!" he ordered. "Won't answer to *Mister*."

Reaching into his shorts, he withdrew a roll of cash and handed it to me. "Almost forgot. Here's the money you asked for."

I straightened the bills and counted twenty-five dollars.

"This is more than I need," I said, offering ten dollars back.

"Keep it. I don't think you're gonna get to use it anyway."

"What do you mean?"

Hemingway frowned, suddenly dead serious. "Listen, kid, it's only a matter of time before Jiménez's man figures out you skipped on him and reports back. The colonel will undoubtedly come knocking on my door. We need to get these photos on the *Anita*. They're not safe here."

The shrill ring of the telephone made us all jump. Hemingway's jaw clenched. "That's not good," he said. He picked up the phone and listened without speaking, his expression growing darker by the second. Then he replaced it in the cradle.

Dorothy and I stared at him in dreaded anticipation.

"Dorothy can stay here. It's time for you to go," he said, pointing a thick finger at my face. "There are men in the lobby asking where my room is. The manager is stalling them, but they will be up soon. Go to the *Anita*. You remember me telling you where she's tied up? Tell Joe what's going on. I'll meet you there. Time for us to go fishing until your ship comes in."

"What are you saying?" I squeaked, the edge of panic raising my voice. "I can't leave! All my stuff is at the hotel. I haven't paid my bill. My cameras—"

Dorothy placed a hand on my arm. "Give me the money, Walker. I'll pay your hotel bill and pack your clothes and cameras. Phil can help if need be. What time does your ship depart?"

"Ah, two," I stammered, my thoughts in disarray. I felt as if I was losing control of the situation. This was asking far too much of Dorothy. I tried to think of what I needed her to pack, relieved that my tickets were safely tucked away in my billfold.

Hemingway cracked open the door to the hallway before shutting it quickly.

"Too late to go that way!" he hissed, his voice urgent and commanding. "They're coming up in the elevator. Go out the window to the next room and down the stairs. The windows are never locked. I'll meet you at the *Anita*."

Blood drained from my head, and the room swam around me for a second. "What?" I blurted, unsure if I had heard him correctly.

"Go!" Hemingway thundered, pointing at the double windows as a flash of lightning illuminated Havana. "Don't be a puff. You saw Jane do it. Now, go!"

"No, no, no! You don't understand. I—" I began, my protests cut short by a sharp knock on the door.

Still hesitating, I looked between Dorothy and the windows. Her eyes were as huge and round as mine must have been.

"This is the police, Señor Hemingway! Open up!" came a hard voice from the hallway.

Hemingway shot me an urgent look and shouted, "Just a minute. I have to find my shorts."

Taking a deep breath, I opened the windows and examined the ledge below the protective balustrade railing. The curtains blew in, rain pelted my face and spattered on the floor.

What the hell was I thinking? I can't do this!

Another hard bang rattled the door. "Señor Hemingway!"

"A minute, goddammit!" Hemingway shouted back. His look told me that I either climbed out the window or he would throw me out. "Go, Walker! Go to the *Anita*. I'll be damned if they get their hands on those photos!"

I don't know where the courage came from that night. It had been a long day: I was abducted off the street in broad daylight, languished for hours in a prison cell, gone toe-to-toe with the head of the Secret Police, and escaped from my hotel under the watchful eye of Jiménez's thug. I was tired, frightened, and pissed off.

Was all of this worth it? What if the photos never left Cuba? Were a handful of photographs worth risking my life?

Then I thought of José de Castro and the sacrifices he had already endured. I remembered the impoverished village where he grew up, the children playing in a mud puddle, and the black, grizzled face of a dock worker who was once a mathematics teacher. How much were *they* willing to risk?

With stiff resolve, I pulled the valise strap over my shoulder and stepped over the railing onto the narrow ledge. Pressing my back against the slick, rain-soaked wall, fingers digging into the smallest masonry joint.

Giving me one last frightened look of encouragement, Dorothy locked the windows behind me.

As I passed Hemingway's side window, I glimpsed him opening his door, where two men waited in the hallway. A moment earlier, I would have been outlined against the raging storm.

I also saw Dorothy sitting on the edge of Hemingway's bed, clutching the end of the bedsheet to her chest in false modesty. The two goons were not fooled by Dorothy's performance and began looking around the room.

Rain beat against my face, and each lightning flash left glowing orbs swimming in my eyes. Half-blinded by the storm, I inched along the ledge, my heart pounding. The wind whipped my clothes, threatening to snatch me from the building and hurl me to the pavement five stories below.

Then, I made the mistake of looking down.

My foot slipped on the wet bricks. A tunnel opened, and the street, sixty feet below, seemed to rush at me. I gasped in sheer terror, scrabbling for a fingerhold and pushing my back against the wall.

Gulping huge breaths of wet air, I clung to the facade, thankful that the storm's noise covered the sound of my 'Tell-Tale Heart.'

Gathering my quickly evaporating strength, I slid sideways the last few feet. Like a thief in the night, I peeked in the window of the adjacent room. Although the lights were off, I could see a man and a woman in bed.

There was no point in being subtle. I pushed against the windows.

They didn't budge.

Desperate to get off the ledge and out of the storm, I exerted more force. The door frame bowed slightly, and the latch gave way with an alarmingly sharp crack. I climbed over the railing into the dark room.

The man in the bed came instantly awake, ready to defend his wife. Before he could cry out or attack me, I rushed for the door and exited the room. Hemingway's angry voice echoed in the hallway, but no one stood guard or impeded my escape.

The stairs were directly in front of me, the elevator to my right. I darted across the hall and took the steps two at a time, circling the ten landings to the lobby. Emerging on the main floor, I paused momentarily to see if any of Jiménez's men lurked in the shadows.

There was one—the same poor sod who had diligently waited for me at my hotel throughout the afternoon. Oblivious to my presence, he stood with his back turned, lost in a cloud of smoke from an inevitable cigarette.

Squaring my shoulders, I simply walked by him, as casual as a tourist would be—a tourist leaving a trail of water on the floor, that is.

Reaching the street, I broke into a steady jog toward the San Francisco Wharf, four blocks away. The rain continued unabated though the storm had passed. The worst of it had beat upon the city while I was exposed on the side of a hotel five stories in the air.

Havana's San Francisco Wharf comprises three piers, each with a large two-story concrete building used to store imported and exported goods. The piers are directly opposite the massive Custom House that stretches the entire length of the wharf.

I jogged past the northernmost pier, also called San Francisco, where the SS *Virginia* would be moored in a few hours. If I was lucky, I would be boarding her without incident and away from Havana forever.

The next pier, Machina, was reserved for commercial boats. The third pier, Santa Clara, was crowded on both sides with more types of small craft than I knew existed. There were gaff-rigged fishing boats, trawlers, and a collection of cabin cruisers. I had no idea which one was the *Anita*.

In one of our lively discussions over drinks at the Floridita, Hemingway had described her as a thirty-four-foot Redwing cabin cruiser. I didn't know what that meant. Many of the boats appeared to be of similar size and had some form of cabin.

I walked partway along the first dark pier before realizing how futile it was. Half the boats were tied up so I could read the name on the stern. The rest faced the other direction, making it impossible to find the *Anita*. Frustrated and frightened, I spun in the rain, trying to determine my next move.

"You lost, kid?" a voice called from the darkness. I squinted into the rain, making out the powerful figure of Ernest Hemingway striding toward me, open shirt blowing in the wind. "Come on, she's here." Without hesitating, Hemingway walked right past me, and I gratefully followed in his wake.

The tide was out, forcing Hemingway to jump down to the deck of the *Anita*. The sound of two hundred pounds landing on the deck brought a shout of alarm from inside the cabin.

"It's me, Josie," Hemingway called out. "Wake up, we have to get underway."

"What the hell, Hem?" growled a shirtless, unshaven man who staggered up the steps from the cabin. Joe Russell, owner and captain of the *Anita*, peered at us as if believing himself still asleep.

From a pile of blankets in the corner, another man rose from the deck, rubbing his chin in confusion. Carlos Gutierrez was the old fisherman who told great fish stories and taught Hemingway the art of marlin fishing.

In short, crisp sentences, Hemingway explained who I was, why we were running from *la Porra*, and our need to be away from Havana.

Having been a smuggler, Joe Russel [19] understood the necessity of evading authorities at a moment's notice. Without a single question, he opened the fuel line and fired the engine. Carlos cast off the lines, and Joe backed her out of the slip. Spinning the wheel, we turned northward.

I stood at the gunnel as we cleared the entrance channel to Havana Harbor, passed beneath El Morro Castle, and entered the Florida Straits.

Before long, the lights of Havana faded in the distance, diminishing like a forgotten dream. My thoughts returned to Dorothy, the risks she had taken, and all I had asked of her. She was an extraordinary young woman with an audacious spirit, yet I seemed willing to walk away. Why, I asked myself. What was there for me in New York? These conflicting thoughts brought on a

---

[19] Joseph Stanford "Sloppy Joe" Russell (1889—1941) was a fisherman, rumrunner, smuggler, and Hemingway's longtime friend who introduced the writer to deep sea fishing. In 1933. he opened a bar on Greene Street in Key West (Hemingway suggested the name Sloppy Joe's), in the location now occupied by Captain Tony's. In 1937, Joe moved his bar to the corner of Greene and Duval Streets where it exists today. Russell died in Havana visiting Hemingway.

deep melancholy, and a single tear ran down my cheek.

"It's a hard thing, leaving what you love," Hemingway said, joining me at the gunnel.

I brushed away the tear. "Havana is the last place I would claim to love," I scoffed.

He gripped the back of my neck and squeezed hard. "I wasn't referring to the city," he said softly. Then, in a much more carefree tone, he announced. "We'll stay out until it's time to meet your ship." He glanced at his watch. "Soon as it's light, we're gonna get you a big one!"

Twenty-Six

THE STEADY THROBBING of the engine, the rhythm of the *Anita* passing from one small swell to another, and the warm breeze caressing my face soon lulled me into a deep, dreamless sleep.

Hours later, as the first pale light of dawn appeared on the horizon, I climbed the small ladder to the main deck, feeling better than I had in days.

Hemingway was snoring away in one of the deck chairs. His chin rested on his bare chest, and his head rocked with the boat's rhythmic movement. Joe lounged in the other chair, steering the boat with his feet.

"Mornin', Bubba," Joe Russell said quietly. In his early forties, Joe's face bore the tanned and weathered complexion of a life spent on the ocean. The deep creases at the corners of his bright eyes and the warmth of his broad smile made me like him at once.

"Good morning," I replied and checked my watch. Five o'clock. "When is sunrise?"

"Should be 'bout forty-five minutes. Startin' to get light now." Joe spoke with a flat New England-sounding accent, yet I knew he was a Conch, born and raised in Key West. "Great day for fishin'."

"Every day's a great day for fishing, Josie," Hemingway announced from his chair. He stood and stretched, hands touching the overhead, making the boat appear too small for his body. "Did you get some sleep?" he asked me.

"I did. I feel pretty good."

"After what you went through last night, I never expected you up so early."

I continued to admire the breaking dawn. "It feels good out here," I said, surprised to say it.

"Damn right," Hemingway said. "Nothing like a new day on the ocean to make you appreciate life."

Before long, the aroma of brewing coffee and frying eggs filled the air, reminding me that I had eaten nothing since a pastry the previous morning—before my abduction and hours spent in a jail cell, before the encounter with Colonel Jiménez, and before my death-defying escape to the *Anita*. I couldn't remember ever enjoying a meal as much as the eggs and toast that Carlos graciously served from the galley. When he offered seconds, I gladly accepted.

"Now," Hemingway said, wiping a spot of egg yolk from his chin with the back of his hand, "we have nearly five hours to catch you a marlin and a two-hour run back to Havana to get you to the ship before two. Sound about right, Josie?"

Joe agreed. "Gonna head into the current so we can run with it back to Havana. Already deep water, Hem, so any time."

Hemingway smiled like a kid preparing to open a Christmas present.

Carlos, who seemed to do all the work onboard, pulled a six-foot fishing rod from its blocks. He inspected the hook and then dug in the bait bucket. "Dead," he said as if announcing the loss of a dear friend.

"That's all right," Hemingway said with a shrug. "Carlos likes to fish with live bonito, but dead bait works just as well. The fish doesn't care."

Hemingway secured a leather harness around his waist and secured the lines to the rod Carlos handed him.

The bait went over the stern and disappeared into the wake. Releasing the brake on the huge reel, the heavy-duty line ran out with a high-pitched whine.

"Now," Hemingway said, his eyes reflecting the excitement he felt at moments like this, "Let's catch a fish."

Six hours later, Joe announced Havana 'hull up' on the horizon. My body ached, my face was sunburned, and my shirt was stained with a mixture of sweat and salt.

Yet, despite the physical discomfort, I was more content than I had been in years. The trials of the past few days were temporarily forgotten, the terror of my escape from the hotel room fading like a bad dream.

With Hemingway's patient instruction, I finally hooked a marlin after two hours of backbreaking, futile effort. As I was about to give up, the line went taut, and a moment later, the monstrous fish leaped completely out of the water, twisting its body in an attempt to dislodge the four-inch hook. Sunlight flashed off its silver belly and dark blue body as its long, deadly bill sought to destroy its tormentors.

Hemingway whooped with infectious joy and smacked me on the back. The only sound that escaped me was that of my lungs gasping for breath. But, at that moment, I am sure my face mirrored the same idiotic grin worn by the other men on the boat.

Despite our initial triumph, the marlin had other plans. It made five breathtaking breaches as I pumped the rod to recover the slack line, then shook its head with immense force, and the hook flew free.

There was a collective sigh as the adrenalin level suddenly dropped. I sat heavily on the gunnel, soaking wet, exhausted, and smiling from ear to ear.

"Sometimes you win, sometimes the fish wins," Hemingway said, helping me out of the fighting harness. "You did all the right things, kid. Don't let it get to you."

While losing a marlin after a hard-fought battle could sink Hemingway into a depression for days, I was satisfied to have the fish go free. It had been an exhilarating and unforgettable experience that left my entire body trembling from the sheer exertion.

The massive bulk of the SS *Virginia* rested against the San Francisco pier, her black hull and white superstructure silhouetted against the sparkling Havana cityscape.

I spotted Dorothy standing beside a taxi among the crowd returning to the ship. She was elegantly dressed in a brilliant white dress with a red scarf on her head and large dark sunglasses. Seeing us approaching the pier, she waved, bouncing on her toes like a schoolgirl cheering for her favorite football team.

Joe maneuvered the *Anita* to the opposite side of the pier, aligning it with a ladder that descended from the pier deck. The boat rose and fell with the swells lapping against the pier as I pulled on my suit coat and slung my trusty valise over my shoulder.

Hemingway pointed at the forward cabin where we had hidden the prints. "I'll send the photos to you when I get back to Key West," he said. "Unless you want to take them now. The coast is clear."

"No," I said, patting the valise. "I have the negatives. It's safer this way. Jiménez's men might be waiting for me."

"All right, kid," Hemingway sighed, extending his hand, "this is it."

Grasping his hand, I said, "There are no words to thank you for all you've done." My voice cracked with sincerity. In just three short weeks, a bond had developed between us unlike any other in my life.

I thanked Joe and Carlos, shaking their hands with heartfelt appreciation. Then, with a steadying hand from Hemingway, I stepped from the gunnel to the ladder and climbed to the pier deck.

"Oh," I called down, "I almost forgot—I'll wire you the money as soon as I can."

"Great!" Hemingway shouted as the boat pulled away. "That'll give me an excuse to visit that girl of yours!"

I waved goodbye. The writer stood looking back at me, casually holding the support post with one hand.

Only Carlos waved back.

I passed from one side of the massive warehouse to the other. The air was heavy with the rich smell of sugar and tobacco. Large burlap bundles filled its entire length, destined for export.

Dorothy stood by the taxi cab, my suitcase and camera case at her feet. As I emerged from the deep shadows of the warehouse, she rushed to me, her embrace fierce and desperate. I held her tight, feeling the trembling of her body.

"Oh, Walker!" she whispered, her voice filled with a mixture of excitement and sadness. "Was there ever such a night? You climbed out a window!"

"I try to show a girl a good time," I said, still holding her tight. My emotions were tangled and raw. Afraid I could burst into tears at any moment, I laughed instead, and Dorothy joined me.

Then her face suddenly fell, and her eyes, shimmering with unshed tears, searched my face. Her lips parted, and I pulled her to me. All the possibilities, the future I knew we could not share, and the days we spent together were enveloped in that kiss.

The moment ended, her cheek, wet with tears, lay against mine.

"Stay…" she breathed.

My heart aching, I pushed her to arm's length. "I can't. You're going to Argentina. Your father needs you. I need to make sure these photos are seen by the world. What we've been through — you and I and José, Hemingway — what we've uncovered — it has to mean something. I have to get these photos to New York, and you can't go with me."

I saw the pain in her eyes and the understanding. "Then hold me," she whispered. "Just a minute longer."

Finally, I forced myself to say, "I have to go."

She nodded, sniffed, and wiped her cheeks with the back of her hand.

We walked to the taxi, arm in arm, her head leaning against my shoulder. Each step closer to goodbye.

"I don't know how to thank you," I said, the words inadequate for what I felt.

Dorothy wiped another tear from her cheek before replying. "There's no need to thank me. You've given me an adventure I'll never forget. Besides, Phil packed all your things. He wanted me to tell you that José is doing better and wishes you a safe trip."

I looked at the ship where the last passengers had finished loading. An officer, dressed in a crisp white shirt and shorts, accompanied by a burly deckhand, replete with an automatic holstered at his waist, waited for any stragglers.

"You've been an incredible friend," I said.

With her characteristic sense of humor, Dorothy scoffed, "That's me, best friend."

"I think Frank wants to be more than friends."

"Hmm," she replied.

"I wish there was more time…" I trailed off, having no words left.

"I know," she said, smiling bravely." She placed her hand on my cheek. "Goodbye, Walker. I'll look for your book. And maybe…maybe someday…"

"Dorothy, I—"

Whatever I was about to say was cut off by the squeal of tires and shouts of alarm. At the head of the pier, a sedan rocked to a stop, blocked by the congestion of departing carts, trucks, and taxis. Two men emerged from the car and ran toward us.

The realization that they were coming for me occurred to both of us simultaneously. Dorothy pulled me in for a last, hard embrace, then pushed me away.

"Run!" she cried.

Clutching my valise, I grabbed the suitcase and camera box and bolted for the gangway, startling the two men guarding access to the ship.

The officer stopped me with a raised hand while eyeing the two approaching men. He understood that speed was of the essence.

After briefly examining my ticket, he stepped aside, and I sprinted up the steep ramp to the ship, adrenaline propelling me forward.

The two pursuing men were forced to stop, thwarted by the officer and the steadfast guard. They pointed at me, shouting in Spanish. The officer shrugged as if not understanding what they said. Faces livid with rage, the men backed away from the guard who had drawn his sidearm.

Returning to their car, they passed Dorothy. One of them pointed his finger at her and spoke. Unfazed, she smiled sweetly, irritating them further. With a final farewell, she blew me a kiss and climbed into her taxi.

The car maneuvered skillfully within the narrow space between the water and the warehouse and drove off the pier.

I remained on deck while the deckhands brought in the mooring lines, and the ship began to move away from the pier.

It was Friday, June 16th. I had been in Cuba for almost a month and felt the need to say goodbye to the city and the people I had come to know so well.

I was comfortable knowing that José would be well cared for. With Phillips, he would be safe amidst the turmoil surrounding Machado and Jiménez. Their regime came closer to collapse with each passing day. Sumner Welles was now ensuring their inevitable downfall.

Hemingway would be true to his word and safeguard the photos until his return to Key West, even though I had the negatives. It was an extra precaution that had almost become a necessity, considering the close call with Jiménez's henchmen on the pier.

I never saw Hemingway again. Yet, during our time together, he taught me a vital lesson that would shape my future photographic work.

I came to appreciate that the essence of a land does not reside solely in its vistas, its architecture, or any remnant of civilization. As Hemingway said, it is the people we pass by unnoticed on the streets, the farmers working in the fields, or the laborers on the docks.

And then there was Dorothy. I knew in my heart that our relationship could not go any further. She knew it also. However, our friendship touched me in a way I cannot put into words.

As the ship gained speed, slicing through the dark blue water of the Gulf Stream, the breeze across the deck increased, and the air turned cool. The few remaining passengers went inside. The deck crew finished coiling the lines and covering the lounge chairs. Soon, I had the deck to myself.

To the east, dark clouds foretold another storm. It would rain soon.

Still, I lingered, watching our wake recede in the distance. Watching until Havana vanished below the horizon.

☙

Afterword

ON AUGUST 9TH, three weeks after Walker Evans left Cuba, the military switched allegiances, aligning themselves with the revolutionaries. This pivotal move led to President Gerardo Machado fleeing the country on August 11th.

A provisional government was established under the leadership of Carlos Manuel de Céspedes, orchestrated by US Ambassador Sumner Welles. This new administration aimed to stabilize the nation amidst the political upheaval.

The *Crime of Cuba*, featuring thirty-one aquatone illustrations from photographs by Walker Evans [20], was published *ten days later*.

Speculation arose regarding potential interference by the State Department in the publication of Carleton Beals's book. However, the truth

---

20 Walker Evans (3 November 1903—10 April 1975) was best known for documenting the effects of the Great Depression on Southern farm workers. In his later years, Evans became a professor at Yale University School of Art. Many critics now consider him one of the most influential artist of the twentieth century.

remains elusive. Despite its success as a bestseller, the book had little influence on Machado's fate or the lives of the Cuban people. The prints Hemingway carried back to Key West were no longer important and soon forgotten.

The following weeks were marked by escalating violence, strikes by dockworkers, and growing discontent within the military. On September 5th, a group of Cuban Army sergeants orchestrated a coup, ousting Céspedes from power and installing Ramón Grau as President. A young and ambitious Fulgencio Batista was at the forefront of this Sergeants' Revolt.

In December, President Roosevelt recalled Sumner Welles from Cuba. Historians give his tenure as ambassador mixed reviews. However, intervention in Cuban politics was not viewed well. Subsequently, as part of Roosevelt's "Good Neighbor Policy," the Platt Amendment was repealed in 1934.

Grau's presidency was short-lived, lasting until January 15, 1934. He was forced to resign by Batista, who had been conspiring with the new US Ambassador Jefferson Caffery to install Carlos Mendieta as the new leader.

Over the next twenty-four years, Cuba experienced significant political instability, with thirteen different presidencies, including Batista, who served three separate terms.

In 1955, Batista dismantled any remaining semblance of democracy, abolished the constitution, and seized absolute control of the nation.

Batista's authoritarian rule ended on New Year's Eve, 1958, when rebel forces led by Fidel Castro entered Havana.

Another supposition, one might argue, is the effect Ernest Hemingway had on Evans and his photography.

In 1936, author James Agee and photographer Walker Evans documented the lives of three impoverished sharecropper families in rural Alabama. Their book, *Let Us Now Praise Famous Men*, was published in 1941 and has since been acclaimed by historians and literary critics for its innovative style. Evans's photos are considered comparable to the Great Depression works of Dorthea Lange, Arthur Rothstein, and Margaret Bourke-White.

In 1962, the photos Walker Evans entrusted to Ernest Hemingway were found in the storage room of Sloppy Joe's Bar in Key West.

Mary Hemingway gave the photos and other memorabilia to Toby and Betty Bruce. In 2004, their son, Dink Bruce, re-discovered the photos and the note Evans wrote to Hemingway, stating that he would have pictures for him tonight and more tomorrow, proof of the basic premise for this story.

An exhibit of the photos and the tell-tale note were the centerpiece of a successful exhibition, "Ernest Hemingway and Walker Evans, Cuba 1933," at the Key West Museum of Art and History.

This novel was inspired by that exhibition and the unknown story of the friendship between Ernest Hemingway and Walker Evans.

To view the photos Walker Evans gave to Ernest Hemingway, please visit:
https://www.abaa.org/images/blog/evans-best1.pdf
Or simply click on:
Walker Evans Ernest Hemingway, Havana, 1933

Following is an AP article describing the exhibit at the Key West Museum of Art and History:

Long-Hidden Photos Unravel a Mystery

CORALIE CARLSON THE ASSOCIATED PRESS

KEY WEST -- In spring 1933, Ernest Hemingway had escaped the Great Depression on a borrowed boat to Cuba, where he fished, drank and gathered material for his next novel, "To Have and Have Not."

With him for three weeks in the bars and bistros was a young Walker Evans, who would soon become known as one of the great American photographers of the 20th century.

But for decades, the tale of their friendship and influence on one another's work remained hidden away in a storage room of a Key West bar.

In those boxes and crates, Benjamin "Dink" Bruce discovered 46 original photographs taken by Evans in Havana in 1933. Bruce just didn't know what they were.

Bruce, together with the Key West historical society, unraveled the mystery of the photographs, a $25 IOU and two Americans working together in the midst of a repressive Cuban dictator, Geraldo Machado.

Their story and the photographs are now on display at Key West's Museum of Art & History at the Custom House.

"It was only a short friendship, but if you look at Walker Evans' photographs and read Ernest Hemingway's writing, it's exactly the same style," said Claudia Pennington, executive director of the Key West Art & Historical Society.

In fact, descriptions of Evan's photos -- including one showing a homeless man sleeping against a wall on a Havana street -- appear in "To Have and Have Not," which opens with this line: "You know how it is there early in the morning in Havana with the bums still asleep against the walls of the buildings; before even the ice wagons come by with ice for the bars?"

Bruce, the son of Hemingway's right-hand man Toby Bruce, discovered the photographs in boxes of artifacts his family recovered from a storage room at Sloppy Joe's, a favorite Hemingway watering hole.

Hemingway moved his belongings to the bar when he left Key West in 1939 with his soon-to-be third wife, and his second wife told him to clear out his things from the house.

After his suicide in 1961, Hemingway's fourth wife donated many of his belongings at Sloppy Joe's to the Kennedy Library in Boston and the Key West museum. The remaining items, including the photographs, were left in storage and the boxes eventually moved to the Bruce family collection.

Among the remaining items -- which included animal heads that Hemingway had hunted, fishing gear and handwritten letters -- Bruce took special note of the striking black-and-white photos of Cuba. They included images of people lining up for bread, bodies with slit throats and a marquee of a movie theater playing "A Farewell to Arms." He took them to Pennington, offering them for display at the museum.

"I said, 'Well, I'd like to get a little more information about them before we just put them up on the wall and say: 'nice pictures,'" Pennington recalled.

In his research, Bruce found a book, "Walker Evans: Cuba," published by the J. Paul Getty Museum in Los Angeles. In it were the same images from Hemingway's collection.

He brought the information to Pennington, and they contacted the Metropolitan Museum of Art, which had the negatives and sent a curator to Key West who confirmed the authenticity of the prints.

The one piece still missing from the puzzle, Bruce said, was proof that the photos were printed and exchanged in Cuba. He returned to his collection of Hemingway artifacts -- a storage room packed floor to ceiling -- and found a letter from Evans to Hemingway.

Written on stationary from a Western Union in Havana and addressed to the hotel where Hemingway was staying in Cuba, the letter said Evans had "some pictures tonight and will have some more tomorrow. Also I will change my mind and take a loan of ten or fifteen dollars if you still feel like that." On the back of the envelope, Hemingway wrote "loaned $25."

According to Pennington, the photos probably came into Hemingway's hands because Evans feared that his negatives would be confiscated and destroyed by Machado operatives in Cuba, so he asked his friend to ferry the photos back to the United States aboard the *Anita*.

References

- *Photos Reveal Friendship of Hemingway, Walker Evans*, Coralie Carlson, The Associated Press, 2 May 2004.
- *The Crime of Cuba*, Carleton Beals with photographs by Walker Evans, J.B. Lippincott Company, Philadelphia, 1933.
- *Cuba, the Crucified Republic: Carleton Beals Indites the Machado Regime and American Penetration*, New York Times Book Review, 20 August 1933.
- *J.D. Phillips Killed in Crash of Autos*, NY Times, 24 August 1937.
- *Cuban Troops Fight Machado's Killers Trapped in Havana*, J.D. Phillips, NY Times, 17 August 1933.
- *Cuba Under President Machado*, Russell Porter, Current History, Vol 38, April 1933.
- *Cuba: August Revolution*, Time, 14 August 1933.
- *To Love and Love Not*, Alane Salierno Mason, Vanity Fair, July 1999.

- *Havana: Autobiography of a City*, Alfredo José Estrada, Palgrave Macmillan, New York, 2007.
- *Sumner Welles: FDR's Global Strategist*, Benjamin Welles, New York: St. Martin's Press, 1997.
- *The Hemingway Log: A Chronology of the Life and Times*, Brewster S. Chamberlin, University Press of Kansas, 2015
- *Hemingway in Cuba*, Hilary Hemingway and Carlene Brennen, Rugged Land, New York, 2003.
- *Hemingway's Boat*, Paul Hendrickson, Alfred A. Knopf, New York, 2011.
- *To Have and Have Another*, Philip Green, Perigee Books, New York, 2012.
- *Walker Evans*, James R. Mellow, Basic Book, New York, 1999.
- *Walker Evans: A Biography*, Belinda Rathbone, Mariner Books, New York, 1995.
- *Walker Evans, Cuba*, The J. Paul Getty Museum Publications, Los Angeles, 2011.
- *"Knocking around between money, sex, and boredom:" Walker Evans, Havana, New York*, John Tagg, Lecture at Yale Center for British Art, 30 November 2016.
- *"CRIME STORY: Walker Evans, Cuba and the Corpse in a Pool of Blood."* John Tagg, *photographies*, vol. 2 issue 1, 2009.

Special Thanks

Alfredo José Estrada, author of *Havana, an Autobiography*, for perfecting the history and feel of Hemingway's Havana;

Philip Greene, author of *A Drinkable Feast* and *To Have and Have Another*, nobody knows cocktails or Hemingway's Paris better;

Brian Gordon Sinclair, the creator and performer of *Hemingway on Stage*, for helping me get Hemingway's voice right;

Bob Pittman, for his attention to detail and expert editing; and, of course,

Sandra López, British Embassy Havana, for historical research;

Bill Seelig, for his expertise with large format cameras and darkroom techniques;

Claudia for her support and inspiration for this novel.

I could not have done it without them.

The Author

CRAIG PENNINGTON is the author of two Caribbean thrillers and three historical novels:

Dead Reckoning draws on his experiences in Key West, Montserrat, and Dominica. It tells the story of Parker's ill-conceived journey to Dominica.

Volcano Wind is a Caribbean caper based on an actual yet unbelievable bank robbery during a volcanic eruption. Parker is back!

West of the Alleghenies is the epic story of Fergus Moorhead, one of Indiana, Pennsylvania's first settlers.

The Heart of the Run is the story of five generations of his ancestors in Scotland and Ireland during the 17th and 18th Centuries.

Murder on the Underground Railroad is a thriller set in 1793 and 1826. It follows Craig's 5X Great Grandfather, newspaper editor James Moorhead, as he investigates the murder of Freedom Seekers in Western Pennsylvania.

All of his books are available on Amazon in Kindle and in paperback.

If you enjoyed *The Shadows of Havana*, please leave an Amazon review or five stars!

Made in the USA
Monee, IL
01 November 2024

69126239R00184